HERMITAGE AMONG THE CLOUDS

Other Books by Thich Nhat Hanh

Hermitage Among the Clouds

THICH NHAT HANH

Translated from the Vietnamese by
Mobi Warren and Annabel Laity

Parallax Press
Berkeley, California

Parallax Press
P.O. Box 7355
Berkeley, CA 94707

LIBRARY OF CONGRESS CATALOGING-IN-PUBLICATION DATA
Nhat Hanh, Thich
  (Am may ngu. English)
  Hermitage Among the Clouds/Thich Nhat Hanh: translated from the
Vietnamese by Mobi Warren and Annabel Laity.
              p.   cm.
  ISBN 0-938077-56-2 (paper): $12.50
  1. Trân, Nhân Tông, King of Vietnam, 1241-1294—Fiction.
  2. Vietnam—History—939-1428—Fiction.   I. Title
  PL4378.9.N55A813   1993
  895' .92233—dc20   93-30730
                                                     CIP

CONTENTS

PREFACE

Thich Nhat Hanh

Although this is a story about the life of Princess Amazing Jewel, she is not separate from her father, who abdicated his throne to become a monk and live in the little hermitage "Sleeping Clouds" on Mount Yen Tu. He was known as the "Noble Teacher of Bamboo Forest" and was the founder of the "Bamboo Forest School of Zen Meditation."

Before becoming a monk, the Noble Teacher was known as Tran Nhan Tong, and he ruled as king over the land of Viet. He repelled the invading Mongol army at the end of the thirteenth century. From the day he was ordained a monk, he lived an ascetic life—wearing coarse cloth, sleeping under a roof of leaves, and going everywhere barefoot. Even as a monk, he continued his work to establish justice and morality in the culture of his people. He travelled to the land of Cham* in hopes of establishing a foundation of lasting friendship and peace between the two countries. Princess Amazing Jewel laid the very foundation stone of this aspiration for peace between Cham and Viet.

As a monk myself, I have tried to recount the story from within the heart and mind of this illustrious monk, the Noble Teacher of Bamboo Forest.

---

* The country to the south of Viet roughly between present-day Hue in the north and Nha Trang in the south.

MONA LISA'S SMILE

Reading *Hermitage Among the Clouds*
Mobi Warren, co-translator

During the months I was working on the translation of *Hermitage Among the Clouds*, I frequently told interested friends that it was a historical novel. This was usually followed by my explanations that it wasn't *really* a historical novel in the sense Western readers might understand that term. It was also a stream of consciousness, a how-to manual on lighting a Vietnamese stove, a celebration of the Buddha's nativity.... I described my translator's dilemma about how to best make this novel "work" for the Western reader. I intended to significantly restructure the book in order to make it more accessible to the Western reader, but couldn't dispel an inner resistance to tampering with the book in such a way.

A struggle was going on inside me, one to which other translators can no doubt relate. I felt torn between my sympathy for the Western reader (wanting to provide a book that could be read with the same ease a Vietnamese Buddhist would feel in reading the original), and my desire to preserve the author's literary structure. Structure cannot be so neatly separated from the meaning of a literary work. For one thing, structure shows us how the author actually thinks.

Students of Thich Nhat Hanh, as well as readers of his Dharma talks and sutra commentaries, often remark how accessible his words are. This has drawn many people to his style of practice. They are therefore puzzled when his fiction requires a different effort. *Hermitage Among the Clouds*, as much of Thich Nhat Hanh's fiction, is told almost entirely through the use of flashbacks. Flashbacks are often contained within flashbacks, strand coiled within strand within strand. Time frames blur. The order in which even basic facts are presented can seem illogical. The Western reader may ask why a certain piece of information wasn't mentioned several pages ago when it was "more pertinent," or why an already stated fact is repeated, seemingly out of the blue? The answer is that ordinary Western concepts and literary conventions concerning time have little place here.

The characters in *Hermitage Among the Clouds* experience everything from within the present moment. Past, present, and future are interwoven and inseparable. Within the space of one moment, a person can simultaneously travel back twenty years, hold a conversation that took place twenty minutes ago in her or his thoughts, and appreciate the sound of a nearby stream. Actually, we all think in this manner all the time. Random thoughts from the past infuse every present thought. The past therefore becomes something dynamic and malleable, something that one can bring into the present moment in order to heal and transform. That healing makes Awakening in the present moment possible, and Awakening in the present moment makes healing the past possible. This is what the character Princess Amazing Jewel, who later becomes the nun Fragrant Garland, is doing throughout the book.

Admittedly, all this moving between past and present is more easily expressed in Vietnamese, a language in which none of the verbs have tenses. There are small indicator words that can be attached to verbs to indicate past or future, but they are often dispensed with since one can understand the meaning through context. It is possible in Vietnamese to move among different time frames with a great simplicity and ease of language. In English, with our required verb tenses, flashbacks can sound awkward and cumbersome. Our very language leads us towards a more linear structure because it sounds and feels more orderly and comfortable. Writers in English who experiment with different time frames often do so by infusing their language with a poetry that can temporarily suspend our attachment to the linear. What can be taken for granted in Vietnamese is more difficult to sustain in English.

A Western novel generally follows the convention of the unity of time, place, and action. Action is structured to take place over a period of time during which the main characters confront and resolve some primary crisis or conflict. Western stories follow a linear time frame in which the main characters remain central throughout the narrative and minor characters remain peripheral. We are so accustomed to hearing and telling stories that emphasize the centrality of certain individuals and the importance of conflict, we don't stop to consider that telling stories in such a way is not the only or even the most accurate way of describing the experience of life. When we confront literature that follows a circular pattern, something in us rebels. We may criticize the author for writing in a confused style when what is really going on is that our concepts of time are being challenged. When we confront a story in which minor characters suddenly command entire chapters while the main character fades into the background, we may criticize the author for digressing, when in fact the author is showing us that the characters are interdependent. They are all reflections of each other, all contained within each other. To separate them into major and minor characters creates a false division. We are equally confounded when the author devotes as much time to mundane, daily life details as to conflict or "the big issues." Is he telling us to look for the miraculous in the ordinary?

Hermitage Among the Clouds moves in circles. One could almost start reading the book in any chapter. I am reminded of Leonardo da Vinci's painting, *Mona Lisa*. No matter where you stand in the room, her eyes always look directly at you. No matter where you start reading *Hermitage Among the Clouds*, you are always in the present moment. Mona Lisa's one-pointed gaze that sees everywhere at once and her mysterious smile have granted her a unique longevity. Many people through the centuries have devoted a lot of thought and debate as to why she is smiling. Others simply look at her and smile back.

It was during my third rereading and translating of *Hermitage Among the Clouds* that I was suddenly able to turn off my Western expectations of a historical novel. And then a light went on. Resistance melted and I fell unimaginably in love with every character and every detail in the book. The Native American author, Paula Underwood, says that every story should be heard at least three times, "once for the left ear, once for the right ear, and once for the heart." She goes on to translate that as "once for the left brain, once for the right brain, and once as a balance between."

In the end, I decided not to change the structure of this book. Retold in a chronological way without all the layers of flashbacks, it would have remained a lovely, gentle, and inspiring story. But there is much more than that to this story. The novel's structure with all its flashbacks, repetitions, and meanderings is a vehicle which invites us to share in Sister Fragrant Garland's experiences of Awakening. She, too, smiles a Mona Lisa smile. It's up to us to let go and smile back.

LIST OF CHARACTERS

AMAZING JEWEL - Princess, daughter of the Noble Teacher, also known as Paramesvari, Queen of Cham. See also: FRAGRANT GARLAND

AVALOKITESVARA - Buddhist Bodhisattva of Compassion, also known as Quan Am

BAO PHAC - National Buddhist teacher of Vietnam who ordained Amazing Jewel

BAO SAT - Zen master who lived on Mount Yen Tu with the Noble Teacher

BAO TU - Queen, wife of King (Tran) Anh Tong

CAM - half-sister of Tam (Queen Y Lan)

DANG VAN - Minister in King Anh Tong's court; with Minister Tran Khac Chung led delegation that rescued Amazing Jewel from Cham

DAO NHAT - National Buddhist teacher of Vietnam who ordained the Noble Teacher

DAWN - nine-year-old girl, novice in Amazing Jewel's nunnery, Tiger Mountain Convent, also known as Young Mountain Convent

DAYADA - son of Amazing Jewel and King Harijit

DHARMA LAMP - novice monk, favorite young student of the Noble Teacher

DOAN NHU HAI - Minister in King Anh Tong's court who initially opposed Amazing Jewel's marriage to the King of Cham

FRAGRANT GARLAND - Amazing Jewel's ordination name

FRAGRANT GLORY - youngest nun in Tiger Mountain Convent

HARIJIT - King of Cham, husband of Amazing Jewel

HARIJITPUTRA - eldest son of King Harijit, ascended to the throne on Harijit's death

HUE - Prince, second son of the Noble Teacher

KHANH - attendant of Amazing Jewel who accompanied her to Cham; later opens up a paper goods shop

KHAN TU - Queen Mother, wife of the Noble Teacher, daughter of General Tran Hung Dao

LOI - Phung's son who attended school at Tiger Mountain Convent; father died in battle

LY NHAN TONG - Ly Dynasty King; son of King Ly Thanh Tong and Queen Y Lan

LY THANH TONG - Ly Dynasty King, father of Ly Nhan Tong

MANH - son of King Anh Tong, later succeeds to the throne as King Minh Tong

PEACE BLOSSOM - nun in Young Mountain Convent

PEARL - attendant of Amazing Jewel who accompanied her to Cham; later married Sinh

PHAP LOA - Dharma heir of the Noble Teacher

PHUNG - mother of Loi who gives birth to second child, Awake, in Tiger Mountain Village

QUANG KHAI - General who bravely resisted the Mongols; father of Van Hue Vuong

RATNA - Champa attendant of Amazing Jewel

SINH - Pearl's husband

STILL RADIANCE - abbess of Tiger Mountain Convent (Young Mountain Convent)

TAM - peasant girl who became Queen Y Lan, wife of King Ly Thanh Tong, and mother of Ly Nanh Tong during the Ly Dynasty

TRAN ANH TONG - Prince Thuyen, eldest son of the Noble Teacher, who succeeds to the throne as King Anh Tong

TRAN HUNG DAO - father of Queen Khan Tu, maternal grandfather of Amazing Jewel; younger brother of Tue Trung; national hero

TRAN KHAC CHUNG - Minister of the Interior in King Anh Tong's court; along with Minister Dang Van, led delegation that rescued Queen Amazing Jewel from Cham

TRAN NHAN TONG - Noble Teacher, founder of the Bamboo Forest School of Zen; King of Viet who repelled the Mongols under Kublai Khan at the end of the thirteenth century; father of Prince Thuyen, Prince Hue, and Princess Amazing Jewel

TRAN THAI TONG - King of Viet before Tran Nhan Tong; paternal grandfather of Amazing Jewel

TRUC FAMILY - parents of Dawn, father caretaker of Tiger Mountain Convent's rice fields

TU - midwife in Tiger Mountain village, attended Phung at the birth of Awake

TUE TRUNG - elder brother of Tran Hung Dao; later became a monk; teacher of Noble Teacher; eminent master

TUYEN TU - sister of Queen Khan Tu, who becomes Queen Mother on Khan Tu's death; later ordained by Phap Loa

VAN HUE VUONG - tutor to Amazing Jewel, son of General Quang Khai; godparent of Pearl

Y LAN - Ly Dynasty Queen, wife of King Ly Thanh Tong and mother of Ly Nanh Tong

HERMITAGE AMONG THE CLOUDS

CHAPTER ONE

AWAKE

Mount Yen Tu, *1308*

Princess Amazing Jewel awoke to the sound of chanting. The novice's voice was as clear as a bronze bell as he slowly chanted the opening verses to the morning service: *"All powerful, all compassionate one of great strength, inestimable joy, bidding us to enter the highest awakening, dwelling in the ten directions, establishing the direct path...."*

Amazing Jewel did not rise, but allowed her body to relax as the words penetrated her heart and mind. Rarely, if ever, had she experienced such peace and joy, and she closed her eyes to savor it. Her breathing was light and soft.

As the novice, Dharma Lamp, began to chant the first verses of the *Surangama Dharani*, the wooden drum beat faster, and his tone changed. His words lifted like a kite in the wind. The drum's single beats blended into a smooth sound that reminded Amazing Jewel of a silken thread floating in the air. The novice began the chant dedicated to the bodhisattva of great compassion. Amazing Jewel's thoughts turned to her father, the former King. She imagined him, up at his Sleeping Clouds Hermitage, sitting in meditation that very moment. She knew that later in the day she would climb with him up to the peak of the mountain. Slowly, she sat up.

It was dark in the room. The flame in the oil lamp on the corner table was no larger than a small bean. Amazing Jewel slid her feet across the floor by the bed until they came to rest in the straw sandals Dharma Lamp had given her. She crossed the room and turned up the lamplight. The room was bare save for one tiny table and a small bed. She covered her shoulders with the woolen blanket from the bed.

It was still dark, but Amazing Jewel could make out the dim outlines of rocks and trees that surrounded the hermitage. She shivered in the cold mountain air and returned to her room, wrapping the blanket firmly around her. Again she concentrated her mind on Dharma Lamp's chanting as he repeatedly invoked the name of Shakyamuni Buddha.

Amazing Jewel's brother, Prince Hue, had brought her to the foot of the mountain in a two-horse carriage the day before. He wanted to appoint bearers to carry her up the mountain, but she refused. Instead, one young nun from the convent at the foot of the mountain accompanied her and Pearl, the Princess' attendant, up to Little Dragon Hermitage.

Amazing Jewel met with her father, the Noble Teacher of Bamboo Forest, and they spoke for several hours. He told her to spend that night at Little Dragon Hermitage. In the morning, Dharma Lamp would lead her to Sleeping Clouds Hermitage. He excused himself, saying he needed to attend to some affairs alone and then ascended the mountain path, bamboo staff in hand.

Amazing Jewel held that meeting, their first in more than two years, in her thoughts. How profoundly her life had changed in just two years! When the young nun announced her arrival, her father came at once to the hermitage gate. Though he was somewhat thinner, he appeared as vigorous as ever. His eyes were filled with joy and a love that seemed to penetrate all her sorrows. His brown monk's robe was faded but not threadbare. Amazing Jewel wanted to run up and embrace her father but she held back. Instead, she knelt by his feet and sobbed like a child. The Noble Teacher helped her to stand and led her into the hermitage. She sat on a wooden chair beside her father, while the nun and Pearl stood to one side. The Noble Teacher insisted on lighting the fire himself. He prepared chrysanthemum tea and served all of his guests. After drinking a cup of tea, the nun joined her palms in respect, and returned down the mountain. The Princess asked

At that moment, a bright-faced novice,
no more than ten or eleven years old, arrived with a bag full of
sutra scrolls slung over his shoulder.

Pearl to join the nun and to stay in the convent until she returned. As Amazing Jewel drank a second cup of tea, the Noble
Teacher asked her, "Has your climb up the mountain made you
tired, dear child?"

"Oh no, Your Majesty, I feel quite refreshed. It is so beautiful
up here."

The Noble Teacher smiled gently. "Dear child, please don't call
me 'Your Majesty.' Just call me 'Father.' I have been a simple monk
for more than ten years. When others are present you may call
me 'Reverend Sir' if you wish."

"I shall, my father. I would be most grateful if, in time, you
would instruct me in Buddhism. I wish to be your disciple, to
call you my teacher."

The Noble Teacher looked at his daughter with singular content. At that moment, a bright-faced novice, no more than ten
or eleven years old, arrived with a bag full of sutra scrolls slung
over his shoulder. He joined his palms to greet them. He was the
novice Dharma Lamp, her father's youngest disciple. Dharma
Lamp was just returning from Stone Cave Hermitage where he
had borrowed the scrolls for his studies. The Noble Teacher told
him to rest a little before preparing a simple midday meal for the
three of them. The Noble Teacher and Amazing Jewel then sat
outside on wooden benches, beneath a roof of leaves. The Noble
Teacher asked his daughter to tell him everything that had happened since she had left to marry the King of Cham.

Amazing Jewel did not need to give her father a long-winded
account. He already knew the events that had led to her marriage,
and like her, he knew and cherished the people and customs of
Cham.

CHAPTER TWO

THE YOUNG BRIDE

Seven years earlier, the Noble Teacher visited Cham and lived there for seven months as an honored guest of the Champa King, Harijit, who was thirty-seven years old at that time. The Noble Teacher acquired a deep understanding of the culture and customs of Cham and developed great affection for the young King, as well as admiration for his courage and intelligence. It was thanks to King Harijit's bravery and keen strategy that the Champa people were able to prevent an invasion by the Mongolian Kublai Khan.

On the day the Noble Teacher departed Cham, he promised King Harijit his dearly beloved daughter, Amazing Jewel, in marriage. The Princess was only fourteen years old, and so he asked Harijit to wait another four years before sending a delegation to the Viet capital to perform the betrothal ceremony. Amazing Jewel remembered what a cold wintry day it was when her father returned. Before departing for his hermitage on Mount Yen Tu, he visited the palace to talk in private with his son, King Anh Tong. They spoke for a long time, no doubt concerning diplomatic relations between Cham and Viet. The former King was invited to stay for a vegetarian meal to celebrate his return. Amazing Jewel and her other brother, Prince Hue, were invited, as well. She remembered how well-versed Prince Hue, by then twenty years old, was in the royal etiquette required for such occasions.

After the meal, the Noble Teacher called the Princess aside to tell her he had promised her in marriage to the King of Cham. Although fourteen, Amazing Jewel was young for her age. She bowed her head in obedience but inside she felt as though the news concerned someone else. Marriage still seemed distant and unreal. She did not dwell on it. But time flew swiftly, and when she least expected it, a delegation of more than 100 men arrived from Cham. They were led by the Champa ambassador who brought offerings of precious gifts for the marriage proposal. That was early in the year 1305. The last of the New Year's cake had been eaten and the Princess was now eighteen.

Faced with the irrefutable fact of her marriage, the Princess panicked. She did not know where to turn. Her mother had died when she was just six, and her aunt, the Queen Mother, was so severe in nature that it never occurred to Amazing Jewel to confide anything in her. Cham seemed strange and far away. In all her life, Amazing Jewel had never travelled further than the northern districts of Viet. She barely knew her own country, let alone other lands. When she was a small child, Lord Van Hue Vuong taught her, "Viet borders Sung to the north, Khmer to the west, Cham to the south, and the Southern Ocean to the east." He told her that Cham and Viet had fought against each other often since ancient times, and that some of the land in northern Viet had once belonged to Cham.

That evening, after receiving the delegation from Cham, King Anh Tong went straight to the Queen Mother's palace to announce the news. Princess Amazing Jewel stood beside the Queen Mother, but her eldest brother, the King, did not speak to her directly. Marriage was an affair of state about which the Princess had no right to express an opinion, although it concerned her intimately. The King looked at her a long moment but said nothing. At last, the Princess summoned her courage and asked, "Has Your Majesty accepted the marriage proposal?"

The Princess looked up at the Queen Mother and caught her severe gaze. Fearful, she lowered her head again, but her brother answered kindly, "No, not yet. As this is a very important matter, I must consult with the royal council before making a final decision."

The next morning, King Anh Tong met with his council, and at midday Prince Hue visited the Queen Mother and Princess to announce that the council had agreed to the marriage proposal. At first, the Prince reported, some advisors vigorously opposed the marriage. They included the official Doan Nhu Hai, a former ambassador to Cham, who was the author of a rejected proposal that the Viet ambassador never bow before the Cham King. Lord Van Hue Vuong, however, voiced strong approval of the marriage. He said, "Our former King's vision has always been broad and far-reaching. He has never made any decision without first weighing it carefully. To our north, the Mongols are confident enough to invade us again. If we do not live in peace with our southern neighbors, it is quite possible that both our countries, Cham and Viet, will fall prey to the Mongols. If the Princess marries the King of Cham, it will secure the bonds of friendship between our peoples and lay the foundation for a long-lasting peace. This is not an ordinary proposal of marriage. Furthermore, we should understand that a commitment made by the former King is not something we can take lightly. The honor of our whole country is at stake. I beg Your Majesty and all the court to give this matter your utmost consideration."

The Minister of Internal Affairs rose to his feet to voice support as well. He, too, emphasized the importance of honoring a commitment made by the former King. He also mentioned how the King of Cham intended to cede the two northernmost districts of Cham as a marriage gift. He pointed out how advantageous this was. Viet would expand its southern borders without wasting a drop of blood. These words won over Minister Doan Nhu Hai and others who had been opposed to the marriage. The engagement gifts were accepted, and the delegates from Cham were told they could return for the Princess in the second month of the following year.

Amazing Jewel could hear no more. She turned on her heels and rushed to her room. Her fate was sealed. Gone was her childhood, those carefree days of laughter spent beneath the palace's familiar roof. All her dreams were shattered. She knew that because she was born a princess she must fulfill her obligations to her country. Her situation was no different than that of her eldest brother, the former crown prince, who had had to bravely shoulder the responsibilities of becoming king. When she had spoken with her father before, she understood the marriage to be a beautiful gesture intended to unite two good peoples. After hearing what had been said at court, she felt more like merchandise being exchanged for territory. The Princess covered her face with her hands and sobbed.

That evening the King summoned the Princess. He did his best to console and encourage her. She lowered her head and listened attentively to her eldest brother, whose duties as king meant that he was rarely able to devote this much time to her. He told her she could take any attendants she wished with her, and that he would personally select a woman of Champa origin to serve as her translator for her first months in Cham. He recommended she begin a study of Champa language, and promised to find an excellent teacher among Champa scholars living in the capital. He also assured her that because diplomatic links between Cham and Viet would undoubtedly grow closer, he would have an opportunity to visit Cham in the coming years.

The Princess asked him about the acquisition of new territory. King Anh Tong replied that it was the Champa King's own idea to offer the two districts as a gift, in order to show his good faith and firm intention to establish lasting bonds of friendship between Cham and Viet. She must not think she was being exchanged for territory. The ceding of the two districts had nothing to do with their father's decision in the past, and it did not influence his own decision now. It was true that there were some men at court who gave their consent to the marriage because they coveted additional territory, but the King himself was concerned only about the Princess' happiness and the promise of opening new horizons of diplomacy.

Princess Amazing Jewel was grateful for her brother's words. Because he had been occupied with affairs of state for the past few years, he had little opportunity to speak from the heart with his younger sister. She treasured one occasion that had taken place six months before when the King summoned her to show her a book of poems and water ink paintings he had done in his rare free moments. He had not shown it to anyone else and asked her to keep it a secret.

She knew her father trusted her elder brother, the King. It was true that as a young man, he displayed a weakness for wine. Though he tried to conceal this from his father, he was finally caught in the act. Amazing Jewel was eight years old at the time. The Noble Teacher had already taken monastic vows and was living a life of meditation in the countryside. One day he made an unannounced visit to the capital. On that same day, King Anh Tong had been imbibing rather too freely. The Noble Teacher searched the palace for his son but, unable to find him, he asked a palace servant to check the young King's bedroom. The servant found him in bed, too drunk to rise. The Noble Teacher returned at once to his country residence after announcing he wished to preside over a meeting of the royal cabinet the following day. King Anh Tong didn't rise until after noon the next day. When the palace servant told him of the Noble Teacher's unexpected visit, the King hurried out of the palace. Not a soul was in sight. Ashamed of his conduct, he went to the royal pagoda. There he met a university student whom he asked to draft a request for forgiveness, before departing in haste for the cabinet meeting at his father's country residence. All the next day, the student knelt in the rain in the palace courtyard displaying the King's request for forgiveness. Though moved by his son's remorse, the Noble Teacher rebuked him, "If you dare behave in such a manner while I am still alive, how will you behave after I am dead and gone?" King Anh Tong bowed to the ground to express his heartfelt regret for his conduct. From that day on he never touched another drop of wine.

He did not, however, cease his late-night sorties. In the early years following his coronation, he liked to sneak out at night after being occupied by matters of state all day. Like his younger siblings Prince Hue and Amazing Jewel, the young King did not like being confined within the palace walls. He asked attendants to carry him in a sedan chair so he could explore nightlife in the capital. Often he invited members of the royal guard to join him. Once, while visiting a soldiers' barracks, they encountered a gang of ruffians throwing stones. A stone hit the King's head and he began to bleed. The King's attendant cried out, "Can't you see this is the King? Off with you!"

The troublemakers quickly scattered. The next day, the Noble Teacher saw King Anh Tong's wounded forehead and asked what had happened. He gave King Anh Tong a good scolding.

As Amazing Jewel looked at her eldest brother now, she remembered these things and felt closer to him. Prince Thuyen was born in 1275 and was only eighteen when he became King Anh Tong. His coronation took place in the third month. In the ninth month their mother died. He knelt beside the Queen Mother's bier and wept until his eyes were red. Amazing Jewel wept, too, but she couldn't help believing that their mother would soon come back to life. Prince Hue was also beyond consolation. He wailed so loudly the Noble Teacher had to gently hold him by the shoulders and ask him to cry more softly.

Their mother was kind, gentle, bright, and patient. Because she was so generous to those beneath her, she was well loved. In addition, few could match her remarkable courage. Once, while she and the King watched skilled athletes fight a tiger, the tiger leapt up onto the royal dais. The royal attendants fled in panic, but the Queen, unperturbed, held up a mat to protect her husband and herself. The tiger roared, but did not attack, and then leapt back down. On another occasion, the King and Queen

*They often played beneath the pine trees
behind the royal pagoda.*

observed elephants being trained. One unruly elephant suddenly charged. Again the royal attendants fled, leaving the King and Queen alone. The Queen did not flinch, and the elephant turned back. Queen Khan Tu was a worthy daughter to General Tran Hung Dao, the general who had defeated the Mongols.

After the death of Queen Khan Tu, her younger sister was appointed Queen Mother and Prince Hue received his full title, Hue Vo Vuong. He was only thirteen years old. Amazing Jewel remembered how funny she thought he looked taking solemn, august steps, dressed in formal robes and a heavy royal headdress. He kept his eyes lowered and looked on the verge of tears. He was a boy who loved to run and jump, climb, and wrestle, but under the Queen Mother's strict care, he dared not appear too rambunctious. Even King Anh Tong was afraid to contradict his aunt.

Once the Noble Teacher said to King Anh Tong, "Court officials once referred to me as a king of great filial piety, but you alone are worthy of such a description." Amazing Jewel remembered how her father told her that her eldest brother was a king who understood that the country belongs to the people, that all the people were his family. In spite of the strict upbringing imposed by her aunt, Amazing Jewel remained fun-loving. Whenever the Queen Mother was absent, she played freely. Although she was a little mischievous, she was never mean-spirited and, thanks to that, earned the palace staff's affections. They never let the Queen Mother know about her harmless antics. Prince Hue took her to play with the children of other nobles, and when their hours of study were over, they often played beneath the pine trees behind the royal pagoda.

When Amazing Jewel was thirteen, Prince Manh, the son of King Anh Tong, was born. The little Prince's mother had already given birth to two sons and was unable to care for all three children. Prince Manh was entrusted to the care of a younger uncle whom Amazing Jewel and Prince Hue often visited. Amazing Jewel loved to cuddle the baby Prince, whom she knew might one day be king. She liked to tickle him to see a tiny future king laugh. All these early memories now flooded Amazing Jewel.

When she was fourteen, her father travelled to Cham on a peace mission. Little did she know how his trip would alter her life. Upon his return, he informed Amazing Jewel that he had promised her in marriage to King Harijit. She knew that according to the ways of her people, a daughter must consent to marry whomever her parents chose. She bowed her head obediently, though marriage still seemed far off. Yet now, she was standing before her brother, her wedding just months away.

For the first time, Amazing Jewel understood how profoundly her life was about to change. That night she could not sleep. In the morning, she asked her aunt's permission to visit her father on Mount Yen Tu. Her aunt ordered a sedan chair for the Princess and allowed her attendant, Pearl, to accompany her. Pearl was the same age as the Princess, and, like the Princess, was tall and slender.

Carried along in the sedan chair, Amazing Jewel's thoughts turned to her tutor, Lord Van Hue Vuong. According to her brother, he had been the first council member to approve her marriage to the King of Cham. He was regarded as the most learned man in the palace. He had always been fond of Amazing Jewel and often told the Noble Teacher how intelligent she was. Unlike some of the mandarins she knew, his approval of the marriage was not based on greed for more territory. Honoring the Noble Teacher's wishes and securing happiness for the Princess were foremost in his mind. Amazing Jewel was fond of her teacher. She knew her father cared for him even more than his own nephews and cousins. Lord Van Hue Vuong was the son of General Quang Khai, who had written a beautiful book of poetry entitled *The Joyful Path*, and who had bravely resisted the Mongol invasion. His achievements equalled those of Tran Hung Dao, a national hero, who was the Princess' maternal grandfather. Tran Hung Dao was also both a man of letters and an accomplished soldier. Lord

Van Hue Vuong was as accomplished as them both and enjoyed the good graces of the former King. The Princess remembered how her father invited Lord Van Hue Vuong to the palace once and ordered the lord's favorite seafood. The Noble Teacher was a monk and therefore a vegetarian, but it gave him great pleasure to watch his friend enjoy his meal.

CHAPTER THREE

QUEEN OF CHAM

The road leading from the capital to Mount Yen Tu was bordered by rows of pine trees which the Noble Teacher had planted a decade earlier. This was the first time Amazing Jewel had ever visited Mount Yen Tu. Because she trusted her father thoroughly, she knew that his counsel would help her in her life. Fortunately, her father had descended from his little hermitage called Sleeping Clouds, located near the summit, to attend to matters at Little Dragon Hermitage, which was lower on the mountain. Thus Amazing Jewel did not have a long climb to find him. Father and daughter sat and spoke for a long time.

The Noble Teacher said, "The neighboring kingdom of Cham is not our enemy as many people seem to think. Cham is an ancient civilization. It has been influenced more by India than by China. King Harijit is a virtuous and learned man. He does not read Chinese, but he is fluent in Sanskrit, which holds the same high position in Cham as Chinese does in our country."

The Noble Teacher told Amazing Jewel that the seven months he spent in the Champa capital helped him to see Cham in a new light. He grew very fond of King Harijit, indeed considered him like a son. King Harijit had inherited the throne in 1285. He married a Princess from Java, named Tapasi, who gave birth to two sons, but then died. King Harijit was forty, ten years older than King Anh Tong.

The Noble Teacher said, "The people of Cham love their King, and I am certain they will love you, too. If you put your heart into it, I think you can create a foundation of lasting friendship between our two peoples."

Her father spoke again, "Look at your hand."

Amazing Jewel held up her left hand. Her wrist was small, her hand smooth and delicate. Her long, tapered fingers were as graceful as bamboo shoots.

"Look at your hand for a long moment. Do you see me in your hand?"

With sudden insight, the Princess realized her hand existed thanks to her parents. Indeed, the presence of her hand was no different than the presence of her father and her mother. She had never looked at her hand in this way.

"Yes, father, I see."

"Not only are your mother and I present in your hand, but our entire country and all living beings are in it. Wherever you dwell, I dwell. Wherever you go, I go. Whatever you do, I do with you. Your going to Cham is the same as my going. I trust you will help keep our two peoples from going to war again."

A strong resolution, arising from love, took root in the Princess' heart. Her father's words were like cool water that relieved all tension and fear. Her anxieties vanished, and she inwardly vowed to do all she could to fulfill the expectations of her father, brother, and all the Viet people. She entered the hermitage with her father, and bowed with him before the Buddha's altar.

During this same visit, the Noble Teacher introduced her to a young monk named Phap Loa. He told her to consider him an elder brother in the Dharma. Phap Loa explained he was still a novice, but that he would receive full ordination on the full-moon day in August. Amazing Jewel could tell how much her father loved this disciple.

Before she knew it, the year was drawing to a close and everyone was busily preparing for the New Year. Amazing Jewel mused how it would be the last New Year she spent in her own country. She was nineteen years old. King Anh Tong surprised her with the news that the marriage would take place in the sixth month rather than the second month as previously planned. She was happy, for this gave her more time to study the Champa language, and more time to savor every hour left in her precious homeland. Because she was bright, she learned the Champa language quickly. Her teacher was a native of Cham and a learned scholar of Sanskrit. He taught her the *Mahabharata*, first in Vietnamese and then in Champa. He was a musician as well and taught her a few Champa songs. He could play the five-stringed sitar, flute, drum, and horn. He also taught her a number of Champa poems and showed her some Sanskrit texts inscribed on palm leaves. They reminded her of the Buddhist sutras she had seen in the royal pagoda.

A large delegation from Cham arrived in the sixth month to escort the bride to her new home. The delegation included bearers of banners, fans, and sedan chairs. There were musicians and maidservants. The Noble Teacher came down from his mountain hermitage to see his daughter off. Amazing Jewel bowed to him, the Queen Mother, and King Anh Tong before departing. She was accompanied by two attendants, Pearl and Khanh, but did not take along her Champa interpreter, for her command of the Champa language was by now sufficient. She took only one trunk of clothes and one trunk of books, which included Buddhist texts compiled by her father, and collections of poetry, literature, and history given to her by her teacher, Lord Van Hue Vuong.

For two months, they travelled by day and rested by night at the plentiful travel stations along the way. These stations all included facilities for cooking. One day as they crossed over a high pass, Amazing Jewel looked down from her palanquin at the breathtaking scene of clouds interwoven with countryside stretching far into the distance. The procession slowed as they approached the capital of Cham and were met by crowds of people. Banners were unfurled and the musicians played sitars, flutes, horns, and drums. The days were clear and sunny.

Here the season seemed a month ahead of Viet, and the rice was already being harvested by great numbers of men and women. When the escort party passed by the rice fields, all the workers stopped to gaze. When the fields were near the road, the people ran up to welcome the Princess as her palanquin passed by.

At last the escort guards announced they were about to enter the capital. Pearl and Khanh helped the Princess get ready. Amazing Jewel felt both apprehensive and curious. She frequently looked out of the palanquin to see what was going on. Sometimes they passed huge towers built on hilltops whose architecture was new and strange to her. She observed that the Champa people did not dress like people in Viet. Many were swathed in silk robes of two or three colors that Amazing Jewel found charming. She saw sparkling white salt marshes similar to the salt marshes in north Viet, but more immense. The rice fields were like the rice fields at home. She saw dams used to irrigate the paddies, and so understood that agriculture in Cham was well developed.

A large welcoming party from the capital met the Princess' entourage. Mahouts, naked save for their red turbans, rode on the heads of elephants which were decked in many-colored silks. Soldiers walked alongside the elephants in brightly-colored uniforms. When the band of elephants came to a halt, the Princess was helped from her palanquin into an elephant-borne one protected by a three-tiered parasol. Music filled the air and throngs of people pressed for a glimpse of the Princess. It was afternoon when the escort party arrived inside the city. King Harijit himself came out to welcome the Princess. The elephant bearing Amazing Jewel's palanquin knelt down, and Champa ladies-in-waiting helped the Princess step out.

Lifting her eyes, Amazing Jewel saw a magnificent palace of unfamiliar architecture, built wholly of stone and brick. Two rows of stone elephants and lions lined the courtyard. Soldiers stood at attention on both sides as their King passed. The Princess joined her palms and bowed her head in the traditional Viet greeting. The King returned her greeting. He was taller than King Anh Tong, athletically built and dark-skinned. His silk robe was embroidered with gold thread. His white silk headdress was decorated with many flowers worked in a shiny material. An at-

*K*ing Harijit himself came out
to welcome the Princess.

tendant standing behind the King shaded him with a parasol. The King turned around to signal the attendants to escort the Princess into the palace where she could be served refreshment.

The days that followed bustled with activity. Bright lanterns and garlands of flowers were hung throughout the palace and city. Great throngs of people attended the Princess' coronation ceremony. It was clear to Amazing Jewel how deeply the people respected and loved their king. King Harijit ordered a stele set up in Posati to record the event for posterity. The celebration lasted three days and nights. Court music echoed throughout the palace. On the first night, a group of actors and singers performed the *Mahabharata* by bright torchlight in the palace courtyard. A huge crowd had assembled. The King and Queen sat on a raised dais, sheltered by a roof. On the second night, a group of singers performed the *Ramayana*. Because Amazing Jewel did not know the story, the King explained it to her during the performance. On the third night, three Champa dancers performed folk dances. Their dress was not as graceful as the garb worn by Viet dancers, but their bare arms, calves, necks, and bellies were decorated with beaded bracelets. Their movements were lithe and supple, especially the movements of their arms. At first, Amazing Jewel found it strange, but before long she was mesmerized by the unique beauty of Champa dance.

The moment Amazing Jewel met King Harijit, she could tell by looking into his eyes how special he was. He was visibly pleased when her first words to him were in Champa. Amazing Jewel had carefully practiced pronouncing those first sentences with her tutor. The King told her that when no one else was present, she could call him by his personal name, Harijit.

Love quickly blossomed in the Princess' heart. Harijit never neglected affairs of state, but when he had spare time, he spent it with the Queen. Because Khanh and Pearl knew little of the Champa language, they were unable to be of much assistance to Amazing Jewel. In fact, they often had to ask the Queen to translate for them. Amazing Jewel requested that her two attendants be given an opportunity to study Champa until they were able to communicate well with others in the palace. The new Queen visited every corner of the palace and inquired about the function of every room. She soon began organizing life in the palace.

The King went on frequent inspection tours to be in touch with his subjects. Amazing Jewel often accompanied him. He took her to see the four famous towers in the capital—the silver, golden, copper, and ivory towers. He also took her to see a large tower he had recently commissioned called Po Klaung Garai with which he was well pleased. The high tower boasted thirty intricately decorated round roofs. He told her he had also ordered the construction of a new tower on the Darlat plateau.

All of the towers Amazing Jewel visited housed the sacred *linga*, an unadorned, pillar-like stone, which was placed on a stone slab called *yoni*. The linga symbolized the male principle and the yoni the female. The King told Amazing Jewel that the linga stone was always placed in the center of the tower. These symbols belonged to the Hindu religion. Amazing Jewel learned that the Hindu trinity consisted of the three deities Brahma, Vishnu, and Shiva. Brahma was the creator god. Harijit said that in former times a large number of his people followed Buddhism but now two-thirds of the people were Hindu. Knowing that the Princess was a Buddhist, the King took her to a large pagoda so she could perform Buddhist devotions.

In Cham, a pagoda was called a *vihara* and the monks wore saffron-colored robes, unlike the brown robes of Viet monks. Amazing Jewel noticed that, along with a statue of the Lord Buddha in the principal shrine room, there was a statue of the bodhisattva of compassion. In Cham she was called Lakhshmindra-Lokesvara. The head monk at the vihara told the Queen that in the ancient capital at Indrapura, in northern Cham south of Cloud Pass, there was a large Buddhist monastery. It had been established more than 400 years ago and, at present, housed 200 monks. Unfortunately, the monastery was badly in need of repair. Amazing Jewel stayed at the vihara to hear the monks chant.

Their recitation was in Sanskrit. She recognized the prayer "Divine Protector," which she had learned by heart, even though the Viet pronunciation of Sanskrit differed greatly from the Champa.

Amazing Jewel especially enjoyed touring with her husband, because it brought her into close contact with people in the countryside. She visited rice fields, salt marshes, silk-weaving establishments, and fishing villages. The coastal waters around Cham were rich in fish, and she could see how skilled the Champa fishermen were. They fashioned light boats which sped over the water. The coastal people were excellent swimmers and skilled seafarers, which explained why Cham was such a strong naval power. Harijit explained that soldiers were paid in rice and clothes. In times of peace, they constructed brick ramparts, embankments, and stone watchtowers to protect the eastern inhabitants of Cham. On their tours, Amazing Jewel spoke directly to fishermen, women weavers, and children. Most people went barefoot, for only the rich could afford shoes. The people dressed most often in a single wraparound of silk. Women and young girls pierced their ears and wore silver rings. Older people wore their hair in buns. Houses in Cham were built of brick washed with lime and were more solid that the rural houses in Viet. The houses of better-off citizens sported sturdy, flat roofs.

Amazing Jewel noticed that many children suffered from eye infections. She asked Harijit to have medicine prepared based on a Viet remedy she knew. She took the eye salve along on all their outings, and whenever she came across children with infected eyes, she asked that their eyes be rinsed in a warm solution of salt water. She then applied the eye balm with her own hands. The King always waited patiently while she performed this task. Amazing Jewel was happy with her new life. In Viet she was rarely allowed beyond the palace walls, and whenever she had visited outlying districts, she was not allowed direct contact with the people or to play with the children.

Harijit told Amazing Jewel that there had once been two ruling families in Cham—the Coconut Clan and the Areca Palm

Clan. For centuries, these two families struggled against each other, each trying to gain the upper hand. Much blood was spilled before they reached a compromise. The Coconut Clan held the north and established a capital near Cloud Pass which they called Indrapura. The Areca Palm Clan ruled over the southern region called Paduranga.

Champa New Year fell exactly two months earlier than New Year in Viet. In Vijaya, the capital of Cham, a magnificent celebration was organized. In front of the palace, royal guards erected a tent which could hold 1,000 people for religious ceremonies. Everywhere lamps and flowers were suspended. On New Year's Eve, the King and Queen sat on a high platform and watched a glorious display of exploding fireworks that sounded like cannons shaking the whole capital. People organized boat races, pole climbing, wrestling, cock and elephant fights, as well as performances of dancing, singing, and drama.

Harijit took Amazing Jewel to see all the celebrations. Surprised, Amazing Jewel thought she recognized some of the melodies she heard. Then she recalled that her teacher had told her that during the Ly dynasty, songs and dances from Cham were brought to Viet. The King explained various singing styles to her. The country people played a two-stringed lyre like the lyre of Viet. Their drums were similar, too. Every night a performance took place in the great tent to a packed audience seated in two circles. The New Year's festivities lasted ten days.

When he was not busy with affairs of state, Harijit sat with Amazing Jewel and told her the history of Cham. From her earliest years, the Princess had a passion for learning, and she listened intently to all the King had to say. Touched by her sincere interest, Harijit found it easy to share his heart's thoughts with her. He recounted how he and King Indravarman led the resistance against the Mongol army before Amazing Jewel was even born. Amazing Jewel was born in 1286, shortly after Viet defeated the Mongol forces. According to Harijit, in 1283 the king of the ruling Mongolian dynasty in China ordered General Toa Do to invade Cham. Toa Do wanted to pass through Viet, but the King—Amazing Jewel's father—would not allow it, forcing them to travel by sea. More than 1,000 ships sailed from Quang Chau to the shores of Cham. Crown Prince Harijit was only eighteen, but his fierce determination to defeat the invaders made him the very soul of Champa resistance. Harijit's name aptly meant "Victorious Lion." He ordered all the granaries to be burned, and then assembled and trained soldiers in the mountain forests. Toa Do's army met with heavy casualties. Mongol reinforcements led by O Ma Nhi were held up at the Chinese-Viet border. Then, in 1286, Toghon, the son of Kublai Khan, invaded Viet. Toa Do was ordered to pull his remaining army out of Cham and go north to support Toghon. Thus Cham avoided coming under the yoke of the Mongols.

In turn, Amazing Jewel recounted the Viet resistance to the Mongol invasion. Lord Van Hue Vuong had taught her this history in great detail, having lived through the invasion and being personally acquainted with all the heroes of the resistance. Harijit was equally absorbed by Amazing Jewel's account and occasionally interrupted her to ask questions. She told him that her uncle and her teacher's father were both resistance heroes.

From Harijit, Amazing Jewel also learned how many times Cham had been invaded by both Khmer and Viet. In 1145, Khmer invaded Cham, occupied the capital Vijaya, and ruled over Cham for four years. Thirty-two years later, Cham sought vengeance by invading the Khmer capital of Angkor. They killed the Khmer King and established rule in Khmer for four years. In 1203, the Khmer King again invaded Cham, and for several years Cham was divided into provinces under Khmer domination. Only after fierce struggle did Cham win back its independence.

Viet, too, had inflicted much misery on Cham. At the end of the tenth century, the Viet King, Le Hoan, invaded the Cham capital, Indrapura. He set fire to the city and destroyed the walls, moat, royal tombs and temples. He kidnapped 100 royal maids and plundered enormous sums of gold, silver, and precious objects. The Cham King was forced to flee south and from that time on, the Cham capital was reestablished at Vijaya in the south of the country. Another Viet invasion took place in 1044. The Cham King was killed, thirty elephants seized, and 5,000 prisoners taken. When the Viet forces reached Vijaya, they captured the Cham Queen and the royal harem and took them back to Viet. Champa civilians were butchered mercilessly, their corpses left piled in the fields.

Cham was invaded again by a Viet King of the Ly dynasty, who conquered Vijaya and took 50,000 Champa soldiers as prisoners. The Ly King ordered his generals to pursue the Champa King until he was captured near the border. He was taken back to Viet, and released only after promising to cede the three northernmost provinces of Cham to Viet. One of the cruelest aspects of this invasion was that all civilian dwellings in Vijaya were burned to the ground by Viet soldiers.

Amazing Jewel buried her head in her hands and wept. She had never imagined that the history between Cham and Viet was so full of sorrow. As a child, Amazing Jewel often heard people talk about war between Cham and Viet, but she had always been led to believe that Cham was the aggressor. She understood the Viet right to quell acts of provocation and harassment along the Cham-Viet border, but never guessed that Viet had waged full-scale invasions against Cham. Perhaps Cham was indeed responsible for acts of hostility from time to time, but now she understood such acts to be a response to centuries of unprovoked attack. The Champa could not easily forget that portions of their country had been usurped by Viet.

Amazing Jewel saw clearly her country's desire to expand its southern frontier. She thought about the two districts given to Viet as a marriage gift, and while her father and King Anh Tong were not influenced by the thought of gaining territory, other court officials clearly were. In fact, the Minister of Internal Affairs agreed to the marriage only out of such motives.

She had only been in Cham a few months, yet already felt like a native. Viet blood still flowed in her veins, but her love of the Champa people equalled her love for the Viet. She saw that their pains, sorrows, and aspirations were the same. Her heart opened to embrace both peoples.

When her father had lived in Cham for several months, his heart had opened, too. He came to love the Champa as much as he loved his own people. He had the heart of a true son of the Buddha, and now Amazing Jewel's heart beat in unison with his. Her heart and her father's were one. Amazing Jewel saw the importance of her mission. She could help build a lasting foundation of peace between Cham and Viet and help both peoples avoid future devastation.

Amazing Jewel wiped her eyes and looked up at her husband. She shared these thoughts with him. Visibly moved, he took her hands tenderly in his and felt as though he were holding the most precious thing in life.

Early that year, the Princess did not feel quite herself. The King summoned the royal physician, who announced that the Queen was pregnant. Harijit was overjoyed. He went out of his way to pamper Amazing Jewel, whom he now loved more than ever. Amazing Jewel wanted to bear a boy who would carry both her father's lineage and the line of her husband. Of course, she knew her son was not destined to become King of Cham, as there were already two princes, the eldest of whom had been sworn in as Crown Prince. His name was Harijitputra, which meant "Son of the Victorious Lion." Both Champa and Javanese blood flowed in his veins. Amazing Jewel had spoken with him on many occasions and found him a most likeable young man. He was twenty-two, and thus older than she, but he treated her with deep respect. In all of their exchanges, the Queen endeavored to sow seeds of friendship between Cham and Viet in the Prince's heart.

Harijit told Amazing Jewel he would be equally happy with a boy or girl. When she told him she hoped to have a boy, he reflected, and then said, "If you give birth to a boy, we shall name him Dayada, which means 'descendant,' 'heir,' or 'one who continues the lineage.' Amazing Jewel was well pleased.

The Viet New Year was drawing near. The Queen, along with Pearl and Khanh, set up an ancestral altar in the palace to make the ceremonial New Year's Day offerings. Viet New Year traditions and customs differed from those of Cham. Amazing Jewel felt homesick as never before. She bid Khanh gather the necessary ingredients for making the traditional "earth and sky cakes," and on New Year's Eve, Amazing Jewel stayed up all night with her attendants. Like three close sisters, they reminisced about all their past New Years, and although the two attendants addressed Amazing Jewel as "Your Majesty," they felt as equals. When it was time to make the ancestral offerings, Amazing Jewel and her two friends prayed facing north. She thought of her father and all those dear to her back in Viet. In that moment, the three young women felt as though they could touch their homeland.

Amazing Jewel promised Khanh she could return to Viet in the summer to be married. Pearl, on the other hand, intended to stay by the Queen's side. She said that making the Queen happy was what made her happy. She felt like a younger sister attending to an elder sister. When the Queen asked her about her own plans for marriage, Pearl only shook her head and smiled. She could always marry a Champa if it meant she could remain by the Queen's side.

Before long, Amazing Jewel mastered the Devanagari script and could read the Buddhist texts in the original Sanskrit. She also learned to read and write the demotic script of Cham, which was written from left to right like Sanskrit and not from top to bottom like the Chinese script used in Viet. She taught Pearl the demotic script, but Devanagari was reserved for scholars and nobility in Cham.

One day after Harijit and Amazing Jewel returned from a tour of Paduranga to see the tower being built on Po Klaung Garai

Hill, King Harijit came down with a high fever. His physicians diagnosed influenza and ordered the palace staff to give him massage. With her own hands, the Queen prepared rice porridge and served it to Harijit. He was able to eat half a bowl, then he broke out in a sweat and felt somewhat better. But the next morning, he suffered another bout of fever. The fever continued to rage, and the King complained his body ached as though he had been beaten. Once again, the royal physicians were called. The King's temperature was so high he became delirious, and Amazing Jewel was filled with dread. The royal physicians attended to the King for three days, but then he slipped into a coma. They forced his mouth open to administer medicine, but the fever did not subside. Three nights the Queen stayed by the King's bedside. Pearl and Khanh offered to take her place and implored her to rest, but the Queen refused. Other physicians in the capital, including ones from India, were summoned to the palace for consultation. They shook their heads. Although the King's symptoms resembled typhoid fever, the proper medicine brought no improvement in his condition.

Late at night on the seventh day of the fifth month, the King passed away.

CHAPTER FOUR

PRINCE DAYADA

King Harijit died without leaving a last will and testament. The royal council assembled and agreed to enthrone the crown Prince, Harijitputra, before announcing the King's death to the people. Early the next morning, the coronation ceremony was celebrated in the palace, and Harijitputra took the title Jaya-simhavarman IV. The King's death was announced, and the capital was plunged into a state of grief. People poured into the palace district. They tore their hair, beat their breasts, and wept aloud to mourn their King—Harijit, the hero of their resistance to the Mongols, the ruler they had venerated for twenty years.

All excursions and parties were cancelled. For seven days and nights, a constant stream of people came to pay their respects. On the morning of the eighth day, more than 100,000 people walked in procession behind their new King to accompany King Harijit's body to the place of cremation. His body was placed in a large palanquin sheltered with a parasol on the back of a white elephant. One hundred elephants followed behind, each wearing a silken coverlet. Soldiers, wearing breastplates of cane, marched on both sides of the palanquin. Another palanquin carried Amazing Jewel and the royal concubines.

According to the customs of Champa, the concubines were to be cremated along with the King to accompany him into the next world. Lord Van Hue Vuong had explained the custom of wife and concubine cremation to Amazing Jewel. The practice of this custom, known as *sati*, originated in India. Lord Van Hue Vuong told her that the custom had long been abandoned by the Viet people, but was still in force in Champa. In Viet, sati had been practiced during some reigns of the Ly dynasty, but was abandoned by the time of the Tran dynasty. Nonetheless, from time to time, there had been royal concubines who chose to be cremated with their King. Amazing Jewel had known this would probably be her fate one day, but she had given it little thought. She certainly had not expected it to come so soon. Because the Queen was pregnant, she would be cremated only after she had given birth.

In accordance with Champa custom, the funeral pyre was erected along the seashore. In the case of a commoner, cremation took place the day after death. In the case of an important government official, cremation was organized three days after death. But in the case of a king, it was necessary to wait seven days. At last the procession reached the sandalwood pyre. Drums and horns played mournfully and the people's laments rose as the bier was set down and then slowly raised onto the pyre. The corpse had been carefully wrapped in a shroud soaked with fragrant oils. Hindu priests began to chant the Sanskrit ritual. The chanting echoed far along the shore as tens of thousands of people chanted with one voice. The pyre was set ablaze to a crescendo of drums, trumpets, and horns. Amazing Jewel could not bring herself to look in the direction of the pyre. She was afraid of catching sight of the royal concubines being led to their deaths. Amazing Jewel perceived all these things as though she were in a dream. Just a week ago she was feeding Harijit porridge, but now his dead body was burning on a funeral pyre. She wanted to weep but could not. She knew that if she were not carrying the lifeblood of Harijit in her womb, her body would be burning at that same moment. This realization shocked her out of her dreamlike state. She felt as if her whole life were shattered, a life she had intended to devote to nurturing the bonds of peace and friendship between Cham and Viet. Amazing Jewel lifted her left hand and gazed at it. She remembered sitting with her father beside the stream that flowed past Little Dragon Hermitage.

She thought to herself, This hand is the hand of my mother and father. In this hand, all my family is entrusted to me. But what has this hand, which will soon be burning on a funeral pyre, been able to accomplish?

Her thoughts turned to the baby in her womb. Will our child be a girl or a boy? She knew she would be present in the child's hand just as her parents were present in hers. She would pass on to a future generation the hand of her parents and all her ancestors. With that thought, she felt she could mount the funeral pyre in peace. Knowing she had brought a child into the world, she would not regret giving her own life.

Amazing Jewel asked herself, "Now that Harijit is dead, what is the purpose of my staying alive?" She loved the courageous King, and he had loved her deeply and earnestly. She found happiness in their love—a love which was short-lived but profound. The child in her womb was proof of that. No, she would have no regrets for her own life, but her heart did ache for her child, who would grow up motherless. He would be reared and educated in the palace of the King of Cham, knowing little about his mother except that she had been a princess from Viet. He would never know the safety and affection of her embrace, never know the fragrant warmth of a mother from Viet. Whose sorrow would be greater—the child's or her own?

Amazing Jewel now felt two searing pains. The first was losing Harijit. Without her husband, she felt her life had no meaning. That sorrow would be burned away on the cremation pyre. Her flesh and her widow's grief, inextricably bound, would perish together. But this other pain, this knowing her child would be without father and mother, burned so deep she felt that even after her body was reduced to ashes, it would remain forever like a heavy stone.

The fire blazed. Horns, drums, and trumpets echoed. Amazing Jewel was aware of shadowy forms performing a ritual dance around the pyre to help send the departed King's soul to the next world. Solemn chanting droned on. Crowds of people knelt before the pyre to recite mantras. Everyone in the land of Cham, old and young, male and female, knew that the Harijit they loved so well was lying on the funeral pyre. The whole country mourned. Some would mourn the rest of their lives.

When the funeral fire died down, the ashes of King Harijit were collected and tightly sealed in a golden vessel which was carried out to sea on a royal boat. Torches were lit and hundreds of lighter craft followed the royal boat as it left the shore. Amazing Jewel was led onto a craft that accompanied the royal boat. Again, the sound of chanting rose. When the boats reached the open sea, a ceremony was performed to release the King's ashes into the water. Horns and trumpets sounded a plaintive lament. As drums solemnly echoed, white flowers were cast onto the sea, bringing the ceremony to an end. The party of boats slowly turned their prows and returned to shore.

Amazing Jewel watched the white flowers bobbing up and down on the currents, beneath the flickering torchlight. She whispered, "Parted forever, Harijit, parted forever." Her boat, too, swung around and returned to shore. She looked towards the eastern horizon and felt the immensity of the ocean. She recited the *Heart Sutra* for her husband.

The King passed away in the fifth month. Khanh refused to return to Viet that summer, saying she would stay until the Queen gave birth. Amazing Jewel grew piteously thin, and King Harijitputra advised her to take better care of her health. He confided to her that, although the Champa tradition obliged the Queen to be cremated with the King, in the depths of his heart, he wished he could prevent it. But not even he dared to challenge the ancient traditions of the kingdom. The people loved her as much as they loved Harijit, but they did not want their King to be alone in the next world. King Harijitputra did tell her he thought he could delay the cremation not just until the birth of the royal child, but quite possibly until a visit from the Viet ambassador. Amazing Jewel thanked the young King and assured him she was not afraid of the cremation. She asked him to ease his mind and expressed her wish for him to organize the coronation ceremony for his new Queen without delay. Harijitputra granted her request. Ten days later, flowers and lamps draped the streets, and the coronation festival began. In just one year, Cham had crowned two queens. The new Queen was the daughter of a high court dignitary. Amazing Jewel was instated as the Queen Mother.

At the beginning of the eighth month, Amazing Jewel gave birth to a prince. He was given the name Dayada, "descendant," according to Harijit's wishes. Amazing Jewel held the baby in her arms and wept as she thought of her late husband. The little Prince was plump and healthy. His black eyes sparkled. Because the King assigned four attendants to wait on Amazing Jewel and to nurse the baby, Pearl and Khanh had little chance to hold him.

Seven days after the birth of Dayada, Amazing Jewel met privately with King Harijitputra. He agreed to send a mission to Viet to formally announce the news of King Harijit's death, and at the same time, to announce the news of Prince Dayada's birth. A mission, led by a high court dignitary, departed with a white elephant to offer to King Anh Tong as a tribute from the baby Prince Dayada. Amazing Jewel sent Khanh home with the delegation, entrusting her with a letter to her father, relating all that had happened and bidding a last farewell. She also wrote letters to her aunt and her brother, King Anh Tong. She wrote them in Chinese characters and sealed them carefully, instructing Khanh to safeguard them and to present them to the King in person as soon as she arrived in the capital. Amazing Jewel gave her some of her own jewels as a wedding gift, to provide the young couple with some funds after their marriage.

Ten days passed before the delegation was ready to depart. Amazing Jewel knew that travel with an elephant would be slow. Even with the greatest of luck, they would not arrive before the end of the ninth month. She half-hoped her father would come and visit her before she mounted the pyre, but she also feared that such a sight would break his heart. She did not know what she should wish for and so invoked the name of the Bodhisattva of Great Compassion, asking the bodhisattva to arrange everything for the best.

From that day on, Amazing Jewel followed the example of her father and became a vegetarian. She arose early every morning and practiced according to methods described in the *Six Daily Practices of Beginning Anew*, composed by King Thai Tong, her grandfather. He had written many Buddhist texts, including the *Guide to Meditation*. She had read the preface to it as a young girl, and regretted she did not own a copy of it now. She wanted to practice sitting meditation like her father, but did not know how. She sat anyway, focusing her whole attention on a prayerful recitation of the Buddha's name.

She also visited the vihara with her attendants to prostrate before the Buddha's altar. This vihara was the largest in the capital of Cham, and was where her father had stayed when he was an honored guest of the Cham kingdom. The monks had all known her father, and they treated her with warmth and respect. When Amazing Jewel asked the monks about her father's stay among them, they showed her his room, the sandals he wore, and the earthenware bowl he left behind for the monks to remember him by. Amazing Jewel was deeply moved to see these things. They told her how much they admired his great virtue and generosity. They referred to him as a *dhuta*, a monk who practices austerity—one who dresses simply, eats but one meal a day, and is unswerving in his practice. They told her that no monk in the vihara, including the elder monks, was his equal in the practice.

When Harijit was alive, he spoke to Amazing Jewel about her father's visit. The Noble Teacher walked to Cham all the way from Viet, refusing to sit in the sedan chair provided by his Champa escorts. Another monk, who knew the Champa language, accompanied him. With this monk serving as a translator, the Noble Teacher offered meditation instruction to the assembly of monks at the vihara. Although the King repeatedly invited the Noble

Teacher to stay at the palace, the monk refused, preferring the humble accommodations of the vihara. Whenever Harijit invited the Noble Teacher to the palace, the Noble Teacher always came on foot. Harijit also visited the vihara several times to see the Noble Teacher. He told Amazing Jewel that meeting her father had changed his life.

He told her that he, like all the Champa people, had grown up believing that Viet was an enemy constantly planning to plunder the people of Cham. Cham was forced to pay tribute money to Viet once every three years, and when the Cham and Viet ambassadors met in the land of Sung for this, they avoided each other's eyes. When the Noble Teacher came to Cham, Harijit suspected he had taken holy orders out of some ulterior political motive. The former King's presence and simple manner of living soon opened Harijit's eyes, however, and it was not long before he found himself loving and admiring the Noble Teacher. The monks at the vihara told the King that the Noble Teacher from Viet surely ranked as a saint. The Noble Teacher told Harijit that Cham and Viet should view each other as brothers. Standing together, they would possess the strength to resist any invaders from the north. The Noble Teacher acknowledged the conflicts of the past, and expressed his hopes that they would never go to war against each other again.

When the Noble Teacher told Harijit, "For as long as I am alive, I am resolved to prevent any conflict between our two countries," Harijit understood the Noble Teacher's true heart. He could see that the Noble Teacher, passing through Cham villages carrying his begging bowl, felt the same love for the Champa people as he felt for the Viet. War between their two countries was indeed a terrible mistake. When the Noble Teacher proposed offering his daughter, Amazing Jewel, in marriage, Harijit understood that the monk's intentions went far beyond diplomatic relations and political motives. By entrusting his daughter to the King of Cham, the Noble Teacher was offering his own heart to the people of Cham. He hoped to ease all the grievances that had accumulated in the hearts of the Champa over so many years. Harijit, too, realized what a precious thing peace was. The Khmer still had designs on Cham. In the past they had devastated the capital Vijaya several times. If Cham continued to pursue war with Viet, one day she would face a two-headed monster. How could Cham survive, caught between a hammer and an anvil? Harijit realized that the Noble Teacher's proposal was the answer to the problems that troubled his heart and mind.

Harijit wanted this historic healing of the breach between Cham and Viet to be as beautiful as possible, and so decided to offer the two districts of O and Ri as betrothal gifts. He met with some opposition at court, but in the end, his ministers agreed to what their King and hero wanted. And so, Amazing Jewel came to Cham. Once she was Queen, border skirmishes ceased. She heard that, at first, certain villages in the district of O refused to submit to Viet rule. Consequently, King Anh Tong sent a minister to O to select a Champa as official in charge. He distributed land to the people and exempted them from taxes for three years, and thus gradually they came to accept Viet rule.

Tragically, the love between the King of Cham and the Princess from Viet was broken off too soon. The Princess arrived in the Champa capital in the sixth month of the year 1306, and in the fifth month of the following year King Harijit died. Her eleven months as Queen in the land of Cham had passed as swiftly as a dream. But it was not a dream. Prince Dayada, whom she held in her arms, was proof of the love between her and the King of Cham.

They had entered the eleventh month. In ten days, Dayada would be three months old. How his eyes shone! He watched the movements of his mother's hand and smiled whenever Amazing Jewel cuddled him.

Dayada smiled whenever Amazing Jewel
cuddled him.

CHAPTER FIVE

JOURNEY HOME

That night while drawing the curtain so Prince Dayada could sleep, Amazing Jewel received news that the Cham delegation had just returned to the capital. All night, Amazing Jewel was unable to sleep, anxious to know whether or not there were any letters from her father and brother. The next morning, the head of the delegation met with King Harijitputra. Later that evening, Amazing Jewel invited him to take tea in her private quarters. He recounted details of his trip to Viet, telling her that they remained in the capital of Thang Long for ten days as King Anh Tong's guests. Before the delegation returned to Cham, King Anh Tong told them that a Viet delegation would be sent in the coming weeks to offer final respects to the deceased King and to attend the cremation ceremony of the Queen. Amazing Jewel was disappointed to learn there were no letters for her.

Towards the end of the eleventh month, the Viet delegation arrived, comprised of twelve men led by Minister Tran Khac Chung. Four of the delegates were Viet monks, sent by the ambassador to offer a special ceremony for the late King Harijit. The Queen Mother, they said, would participate in the traditional Viet Buddhist ceremony. After the rite was completed, Amazing Jewel would ascend the cremation pyre. Both ceremonies were to take place by the seashore in accordance with Champa custom. King Harijitputra gave his approval for setting up an altar to the late King alongside the Queen's funeral pyre. The ceremony was to take place on the full moon day of the twelfth month.

Amazing Jewel received Minister Tran Khac Chung for tea. Although she was eager to ask about events in her homeland, she did not think it proper to do so in the presence of her Champa attendants. She found something unnatural about Minister Chung's demeanor. He was certainly polite and respectful, but there was something about his behavior that unsettled Amazing Jewel. Minister Chung told her there were no letters for her from either her father or King Anh Tong. Amazing Jewel sobbed alone in her room that night. She wondered how her father and brother could be so indifferent to her plight. Or perhaps Khanh had never delivered the letters she wrote?

The day of the cremation arrived. King Harijitputra and Amazing Jewel were conveyed by elephant palanquin to the seashore. Amazing Jewel wore robes which a Queen Mother of Cham reserved for the most solemn of rituals. Accompanying Amazing Jewel in the palanquin were Pearl and her Champa attendant named Ratna. They held Prince Dayada, who was swathed in pink silk. An altar of offerings for the former King had been set up with great ceremony. Banners were hoisted to the sound of musical instruments. The pyre, built entirely of sandalwood, was ready. Nearly 10,000 people gathered along the shore. Amazing Jewel was helped into a small boat together with the four monks and her two attendants to perform the Viet ceremony for the former King some distance from shore. They would then return to make offerings at the altar. The leader of the Viet delegation asked that Prince Dayada be allowed to board the boat with his mother, but King Harijitputra would not consent. He ordered the Prince's palanquin be carried alongside his own.

Hardly had the Queen's vessel left shore, when the monks began lighting incense and chanting. The familiar sound filled Amazing Jewel with longing for her homeland. Tears filled her eyes. Pearl covered her face and wept, too. The boat passed ever farther from shore beneath the blinding blaze of the sun. When they were well out at sea, the four Champa seamen in the boat brought it to a standstill to enable the monks to complete their prayers. Suddenly, as if from nowhere, four light boats appeared, each carrying four or five seamen. Amazing Jewel noticed they were Viet seamen. Quick as a flash, they encircled Amazing Jewel's boat and leapt aboard her craft.

The four Champa seamen were immediately overpowered. Amazing Jewel, Pearl, Ratna, and the four monks were swiftly transferred to the other boats. The Champa seamen's hands were bound and they were laid face down in the bottom of their boat. Just then another small boat from the mainland pulled up. Amazing Jewel saw it carried Minister Chung and his retinue. They, too, boarded one of the lighter craft. Amazing Jewel understood then that King Anh Tong had charged Minister Chung to organize her rescue. Minister Chung had kept his plan well concealed. She guessed not even the Viet monks had been informed. Amazing Jewel and her attendants sat without saying a word. Pearl appeared to understand what was happening, but Ratna looked dazed and frightened. Amazing Jewel squeezed her hand to assure her she had nothing to fear. The seamen kept rowing with all their might, flying over the waves like arrows. Suddenly, Amazing Jewel noticed a large ship appear which would no doubt return her to Viet. The seamen called out to one another and rowed ever faster, until they reached the ship. Sailors lowered a rope ladder and the transfer of the passengers from the small craft began. Two sailors above and two below helped boost Amazing Jewel up. She was led down into the hold, where Minister Chung and another court minister bowed in greeting.

Ratna, Pearl, and the four monks were also brought on board. Amazing Jewel and her two attendants were provided a separate cabin. Looking out, Pearl informed Amazing Jewel that all the sails had been hoisted and were billowing in the wind. The sailors were ordered to sail as fast as possible in order to escape any Champa chase.

While talking to Minister Chung later that afternoon, Amazing Jewel learned that King Anh Tong had indeed delegated him and the other minister on board to find some way to rescue her and bring her back together with Prince Dayada. Before setting out from Viet, the two ministers drew up a plan of action. They started out on foot early in the tenth month until they reached one of the new districts ceded by Cham. There they made their intentions known to the Viet governor who helped them acquire the large vessel, the four lighter craft, and the skilled seamen. The second minister was responsible for bringing the boats out from Thuan An estuary to meet the Queen at sea. He sent a Champa seaman to link up with the first minister, in order to coordinate their efforts. However, their plan had not been wholly successful, because they had to leave without the little Prince.

After the initial surprise and relief of the rescue, Amazing Jewel was flooded with conflicting emotions. She knew it was not within her power to decide whether or not she would take part in this plan. It had already been decided at court and she had no choice but to comply. Even though she had been spared the funeral pyre, something deep within her heart broke. She had been prepared to die, even looking forward to ending her widow's grief. No doubt the rescue would be felt by the Champa as an insult, and feelings of trust between Cham and Viet would wither. She was sure her father had not been informed of the plan. If she had been willing to undergo immolation in order to preserve friendly relations between their peoples, she knew her father would have accepted the bitter pain of losing a daughter in order to assure peace. Her brother Anh Tong had been influenced, no doubt, by his two ministers as well as by his desire to save his sister. She knew that these ministers despised the Champa and desired to annex all of Cham. They were blind to the possibility of brotherly love between the two countries.

With a sudden start, Amazing Jewel realized that King Harijit-putra must have known about the rescue plan, but feigned ignorance to allow her to escape. The very fact that he ordered Prince Dayada be carried in a palanquin alongside his own was adequate evidence. He could allow Amazing Jewel to return to Viet, but not the Champa Prince. The leader of the Viet delegation may have thought he had deceived the King, but in truth, the King allowed him to carry out his plan. Amazing Jewel looked out at the expanse of sea and sky. No Champa boat pursued them. She thought of the four Champa seamen lying in the bottom of their boat and hoped they had managed to untie themselves and return to shore. She thought, too, of the throngs of people waiting beside the funeral pyre. She was gripped by a sudden and tight pain. She thought of her son, Dayada, that part of her heart abandoned in the land of Cham.

The boat sailed without mishap throughout that night and all the next day. The following night, a violent wind snapped the mast in two. All night long, sailors bravely struggled to keep the boat from capsizing. Ratna remained calm, but Pearl clung to Amazing Jewel in near hysterics. In the morning, they managed to guide the boat into a bay to shelter it from the gales. For seven days and nights, the storm raged. The boat was too damaged to journey any farther, and so two seamen were sent ashore to purchase materials to repair the ship, and at the same time to bring back fresh water and additional provisions. Luckily, the sailors on board spoke Champa, and because their boat was a Champa vessel, they aroused no suspicion among the local people.

For nearly a month, the boat lay anchored before repairs were complete. At last, the second minister lifted anchor and after a day's sailing, they reached the Thuan estuary. Two days later everyone disembarked. They were in the territory recently acquired by Viet and the majority of the people were Champa. Amazing Jewel and her two attendants disguised themselves as ordinary travellers. Minister Chung made plans to send men back to Vijaya to find means to capture Prince Dayada. He said he could not return home before completing the entire task entrusted to him by King Anh Tong. The Queen Mother was now safely across the frontier. He must now find a way to bring the Prince across, too. He spoke to the local Viet governor about his plans. He intended to send Champa spies, secretly loyal to Viet, who would not arouse suspicion.

Amazing Jewel knew there was nothing she could say to persuade the minister to abandon his plan to kidnap the baby Prince.

Her own emotions were in conflict. She loved her child and longed to hold him in her arms. At the same time, she knew that kidnapping the Prince was an act of provocation. Prince Dayada belonged to the royal Champa family. She had never thought otherwise. If the Viet court gave orders to kidnap the Prince, the Champa would be convinced that the people of Viet were dishonest tricksters who could never be trusted. Amazing Jewel could not bear such a thought, yet she knew that her opinion was of little account in a society where women held no sway in political decisions. She felt no one could understand all she was feeling now, save her father.

In the second month, a cargo ship departed from the Thuan estuary with eight Champa on board with orders to go to Vijaya and kidnap the Prince. Amazing Jewel felt torn inside. She was against the plan to capture Prince Dayada, and yet she harbored a strong hope that the expedition would succeed. She longed to experience the happiness of being a mother again. At first she was angry with herself for holding such a hope, because it made her feel like an accomplice in a treacherous act. She struggled, trying to expel the hope from her heart and mind, but the more she tried to repress the feeling, the stronger it grew. At last, she had to recognize that the feeling was stronger than she was. She chastised herself, saying she was a woman, and therefore weak, knowing it was only a false excuse. She was indeed fully a woman, but that hardly made her weak. She suffered because of what she was—the mother of a child.

Six weeks passed with no news of the cargo ship. Anxious, the minister sent another mission with a different plan of action. This time they were to go overland. Again, six weeks passed, with still no news from either delegation. It was obvious both missions had failed. Two weeks later, the minister decided to abandon the plan to kidnap Prince Dayada. Three palanquins were immediately prepared for Amazing Jewel and the ministers to return to the Viet capital. The party consisted of twelve people, including Pearl

Amazing Jewel gazed at her homeland
with new eyes.

and Ratna. The four monks had already set off for the capital before the feast of the Buddha's nativity.

For thirty days the palanquin travelled. The land of Viet spread before them like an exquisite tapestry. Amazing Jewel gazed at her homeland with new eyes. Every view of gorge or river reminded Amazing Jewel of the people and countryside of Cham. The people of Cham were as much a part of her now as the people of Viet. Both peoples were familiar with hard toil. Both possessed strength and endurance. Both thirsted for peace. As Amazing Jewel looked at thatched cottages half-concealed by bamboo thickets, at farmers plowing their rice fields, and at children riding on the backs of water buffalo, she longed to throw off her regal duties and live a simple country life. She wanted to be born into a new life as a simple rural woman. Perhaps her father could help her fulfill such a wish?

On the tenth day of the eighth month, they reached the capital, and Amazing Jewel was received by King Anh Tong and Prince Hue. They informed her that their aunt, the Queen Mother, had taken religious vows four months earlier at Bao An Pagoda and was now practicing in a small hermitage in the north of the country. Amazing Jewel also learned that it was King Anh Tong's own plan to have her rescued and brought home. As she had guessed, their father had not been informed. After a day's rest to recover her strength, Amazing Jewel expressed her desire to visit her father on Mount Yen Tu, after which she would also pay a visit to the Queen Mother.

CHAPTER SIX

DHARMA LAMP

Mount Yen Tu, *1308*

All thoughts about the events of the past two years faded, as Amazing Jewel returned her awareness to the present moment. Dharma Lamp was no longer chanting, and Little Dragon Hermitage was immersed in a deep stillness. In the space of a few moments, Amazing Jewel felt as if she had relived her entire life. Indeed, she felt as though she had lived through countless centuries. She was still only twenty-one years old yet had experienced so many anxieties, fears, and disappointments. The great weariness she felt upon waking was now replaced with an inexplicable peace and joy. Her heart experienced perfect equanimity. She had never felt this way before, but having experienced it once, she knew she could experience it again, even many times. She had been ready to lay her body on a funeral pyre. Willing to face death, there was nothing now that could cause her fear. Perhaps that was the reason she could now savor such calm and joy. She knew very little about Buddhist meditation but was sure that the peace and joy fostered by meditation was the same as what she now felt.

Amazing Jewel looked up at the ceiling, dark with night shadows, and listened intently. Both within and without her, all was still and quiet. In the darkness, she smiled. That smile was a miracle. She had never smiled in quite that way before. It was not a smile meant for anyone but herself. It remained on her lips as she listened to the sound of her calm and gentle breathing. She told herself not to lose a second of this precious peace by dwelling on any memories or anxieties.

Dharma Lamp clapped the cymbals twice. The crisp yet solemn sound announced daybreak. Amazing Jewel rose slowly. She opened the door and walked to the shrine room.

Dharma Lamp addressed her courteously, "Please, My Lady, have some rice porridge. Afterwards, I will escort you up to Summit's Rest Hermitage."

Amazing Jewel sat down. On the table were set two bowls of thick, brown rice porridge, a plate of pickled cabbage, a small dish of soy sauce, and two pairs of chopsticks. The young novice joined his palms to say grace and then held up his bowl and slowly began to eat in silence. Amazing Jewel did the same. She would never have expected brown rice porridge to taste so delicious. When Dharma Lamp finished eating, he joined his palms in silent grace again, and served Amazing Jewel a bowl of tea. It had been so long since she'd had tea brewed with ginger. How warm it made her feel!

As they walked out into the morning light, mist still cloaked the distant trees. Dharma Lamp pointed out the shape of the mountain ridge alongside Little Dragon Hermitage and said, "You see, My Lady, how the hill is shaped like a unicorn? That's why this hermitage is also called Unicorn Hermitage."

Amazing Jewel agreed that it did indeed look like a unicorn. She glanced back at the hermitage and saw the stream of water flowing past the pine trees. Pebbles and stones of varied sizes lined its banks. Amazing Jewel recalled the afternoon she sat with her father by the bank of the same stream on those very stones, shortly before she left for Cham. That day now seemed no more distant than yesterday afternoon.

They followed the path up the mountain. The path crossed many streams, over which timber bridges had been built. After crossing the ninth stream, they found themselves facing the towering mountain peak. At its foot was a stretch of white sand, washed down the peak by the rains of many seasons. The novice told Amazing Jewel that whenever King Anh Tong paid a visit to the Noble Teacher, he always stopped at this spot to rest.

Dharma Lamp led Amazing Jewel around another pine-covered hill and through another wooded area, to reach a large stream of red water. Dharma Lamp explained that the water flowed through a forest of ironwood trees and turned red. Amazing Jewel looked at the large rocks that lined the streambed. Looking up, she saw thousands of towering pine trees. They entered the pine forest and walked until they reached Stone Cave Hermitage, built entirely of blue stones found near the site. The novice told Amazing Jewel that it was here where the Noble Teacher composed *Words from the Stone Cave*. He said that the Noble Teacher rarely stayed at Stone Cave anymore, preferring Sleeping Clouds Hermitage. The path became more difficult to follow, but the view was breathtaking. They passed through dense patches of forest until they emerged into a sunny expanse. After another hike, they reached a slope covered with trees.

The novice said, "My Lady, why don't we sit here awhile to rest our tired feet? This place is called Cool Shade. The Noble Teacher often comes to sit and rest here. King Anh Tong likes to stop here, too." The novice pointed to a little thatched hermitage off in the distance, half-hidden by trees. "That is Center Stone Hermitage. My elder brother in the Dharma, Phap Loa, once stayed there for a solitary retreat."

Amazing Jewel bid Dharma Lamp sit beside her on the tree trunk set out especially for travellers. She asked him, "Dharma Lamp, who told you to call me 'My Lady'?"

The novice replied, with great respect, "My Lady, no one told me to, but yesterday I heard Miss Pearl call you that, so I thought it proper to address you in the same way."

Amazing Jewel smiled. So he was copying Pearl!

"When you call me 'My Lady,' it sounds so formal. Did you know that I am the Noble Teacher's daughter?"

"Yes, My Lady."

"Well, since you are the spiritual son of the Noble Teacher, that makes us brother and sister. I would prefer you call me 'Sister'."

The novice lowered his head, "I don't think I would dare, My Lady."

"Why not? It is true I am your sister. I am going to study meditation with the Noble Teacher, too. That way, I will be his spiritual child, as well. I don't like being called 'My Lady.' Please call me 'Sister,' as you are my younger brother."

The novice lifted his head and looked at the famous Princess. Lowering his head again, he replied softly, "I will try."

"Dharma Lamp, how long have you been a novice?"

"My Lady—I mean Sister—I have been a novice for just two years."

"You chant beautifully. You have such a clear voice. I am sure the Noble Teacher loves you very much."

"Yes, he does love me. I am only twelve years old, but he allowed me to write a dedication to *Record of the Eminent Master Tue Trung*. It has just been published, Sister, and I have two copies. I will give you one."

"Did anyone else write a dedication for the book?"

"Yes. First the Noble Teacher did, and then six of his ordained disciples. My dedication was at the end. Everyone wrote so beautifully, except me, Sister. Still, the Noble Teacher allowed my poor words to be included."

"What did you write? Can you recite it for me?"

"I wrote, 'The Eminent Master Tue Trung was a bodhisattva, born into the Tran royal family. He was the elder brother of the national hero Tran Hung Dao. In childhood he was a dutiful son and fulfilled his father's expectations. Twice, when his country was in great danger, he helped prevent war. After that, he devoted his life to practicing meditation. Forsaking worldly goods, he journeyed on foot from place to place.' Pretty bad, don't you think, Sister?"

"On the contrary, you write very well. Tell me, why do you want to be a monk?"

"I want to be just like my elder brother in the Dharma, Phap Loa."

"And what is so special about Phap Loa?"

"Phap Loa is the Noble Teacher's Dharma heir. It will be his responsibility to preserve and propagate the Noble Teacher's true teaching. He is even more important than Bao Sat, Sister. At the beginning of the year, I accompanied the Noble Teacher when he stayed at Bao An Temple, and I was present at the ceremony when he gave transmission to Phap Loa. It was a very formal ceremony, Sister. Shall I tell you about it?"

Amazing Jewel enjoyed talking to Dharma Lamp. It was especially lovely to hear his young voice pronounce Buddhist terms like "true teaching," "transmission," and "formal ceremony." She nodded, "Yes, please tell me."

"On New Year's morning, after we chanted the morning liturgy, the Noble Teacher accompanied Phap Loa to the shrine room to bow to the Buddha. Afterwards, the whole assembly had breakfast. They then dressed in ceremonial robes and went to the Dharma hall. The gong and ritual music sounded so majestic, Sister. While the music was being played, the royal carriage arrived along with many of the King's attendants. Since the King is the highest layperson in the land of Viet, there was a throne set up for him in the hall. Prince Hue and other court officials stood in the courtyard. Prince Hue is your brother, too, isn't he?"

"Yes, he is."

"The Noble Teacher went up on the dais to give a Dharma talk. When he was finished, he stepped down and led Phap Loa by the hand up onto the dais. He asked him to be seated, and then joined his palms and faced Phap Loa. In a most ceremonious way, he asked after Phap Loa's health. After Phap Loa gave his reply, the Noble Teacher took his own religious robe and gave it to Phap Loa to put on. Then the Noble Teacher sat down to listen to Phap Loa give a Dharma talk. When Phap Loa concluded his teaching, the Noble Teacher stood up. Facing the King, ministers, and all the assembly, he said that from that day on, the care of Bao An Temple and all the hermitages on Mount Yen Tu was transferred to Phap Loa. Phap Loa was his Dharma heir and would be the second lineage holder of the Bamboo Forest School. After that, everyone stood up and bowed to Phap Loa."

Amazing Jewel looked at Dharma Lamp and smiled. "If I were you, I would not long to be like Phap Loa. To be the lineage holder of a meditation school is a weary task. There are so many things to take care of. I would prefer to be like you. Here there is calm and freedom from all cares. Anyway, the Noble Teacher surely loves you as much as he loves Phap Loa. Tell me, why are so few people on the mountain now? Where have all the other monks gone?"

"They have all gone down the mountain as requested by the Noble Teacher. Master Bao Sat is the only one left, up at his Violet Clouds Hermitage. This past summer the Noble Teacher spent the rainy season retreat in Duc La with more than 200 monks. He gave commentaries on the *Torch of Transmission* throughout the retreat period, and on the full moon day of the seventh month, after the practice of confessions, he performed a ceremony to hand over the charge of Duc La Temple to Phap Loa. On the day after the full moon, the Noble Teacher returned here and stayed at Violet Clouds. He invited Phap Loa to stay with him to receive a private teaching on the *Torch of Transmission*. Two weeks later, he sent the other monks down the mountain, keeping only Master Bao Sat with him. He told Master Bao Sat that he wished to visit all the sacred places on Mount Yen Tu with Bao Sat while no one else was on the mountain. That is why there are only three of us here now—the Noble Teacher, Master Bao Sat, and myself."

Amazing Jewel thought about her father, now fifty years old. He was no longer young, but still shouldered many responsibilities. Though his worldly work was completed, he now had his religious work. She was happy to learn her father had entrusted the mountain hermitages to Phap Loa.

Amazing Jewel was twelve years old when her father left home to become a monk. She still remembered the day, and how moved the kingdom was. The Queen Mother and palace staff wept when they bid him farewell at the foot of Mount Yen Tu. Many could not bear to return to the palace without him, and so built a shelter at the foot of the mountain and remained there. The Noble Teacher did not ask them to leave. As a result, two villages were founded. Some years later, a convent was built at the foot of the mountain, as well, to provide a place for women to practice Buddhism as nuns.

The day the Noble Teacher left the palace, the abbot of Bao An Temple burned his left arm off as an offering. He said, "The decision of our King to follow the Way and make the sun of the Dharma shine is a great and unprecedented occasion for our country." News spread throughout the capital about how the abbot placed his arm over a candle flame for hours, burning it from hand to elbow. The whole time, his face remained relaxed and calm. Amazing Jewel had asked the Queen Mother's permission to go to Bao An, and witnessed the sight for herself.

Amazing Jewel knew her father had studied Buddhism with the Eminent Master Tue Trung, who was also her maternal uncle. Master Tue Trung was considered by all as having attained the Great Awakening. His understanding of the sutras was unsurpassed. The Eminent Master died before the Noble Teacher took monastic orders, and so the National Teacher, the Venerable Dao Nhat, performed the ordination ceremony. The Noble Teacher had lived in a palace embellished with gold and precious gems, but now followed the life of a homeless monk. He wore only a patchwork robe, slept under simple thatched roofs on Mount Yen Tu, and ate and drank simply. He received the Buddhist title "Dhuta" which refers to one who has entered the path of monastic practice. Others, who revered him, called him "Noble Dhuta." Even after spending ten years on the mountain, he had not founded any temple. He and his dozen or so disciples practiced in a dozen tiny thatched-roof hermitages, which included Violet Clouds, Little Dragon, and Sleeping Clouds.

The thought of Sleeping Clouds made Amazing Jewel stand up. She felt rested. Dharma Lamp stood up, too. They crossed the rough forest and climbed for a spell, before reaching the hermitage. They did not see Noble Teacher, and Dharma Lamp said he must be meditating at Samadhi Hermitage close by. He spoke softly to Amazing Jewel while pointing to a tiny hermitage partially hidden behind some pine trees.

"The teacher meditates over there. We must not go near or we might disturb him. Here, let me show you around." Dharma Lamp led Amazing Jewel to a tiny hut built in a rocky crevice.

He said, "This is called One-Roof Hermitage, because, as you can see, it only has one roof. The teacher often sits here to read sutras and other texts. It is cool and quiet here, Sister. Teacher sits in the Samadhi Hermitage several times a day to meditate. When he is finished, I will show it to you. Dragon Stream is nearby, and there is a beautiful waterfall, Sister. The water tumbles down from way up high. The stream forms the tail of a dragon, and the hermitage built in the rock cleft forms the dragon's head. Sleeping Clouds Hermitage is the dragon's back. Come over here and take a look. If you stand in front of Sleeping Clouds and look down, you can see the whole mountain with all its rivers and streams winding down. See how beautiful it is?"

Amazing Jewel looked down. The view was so beautiful and imposing it made her spirit light. She could have spent days in that very spot.

"Some mornings when you wake up, mist covers this area and it is like sitting on a cloud, Sister."

Amazing Jewel smiled and said, "No wonder the mountain peak has been given the name Bed of Clouds." No sooner had she spoken than she heard the sound of footsteps on the dry leaves behind her. She turned around and saw her father, smiling as he approached. Dharma Lamp joined his palms and lowered his head in respect. Amazing Jewel did the same.

The Noble Teacher said, "My children, I did not expect you so early!" He led them both into the little hermitage. The novice began to make preparations for tea, but the Noble Teacher stopped him.

"You needn't make any tea just now. We will walk on up to Violet Clouds first. I have prepared a handful of rice and a small packet of roasted, salted sesame seeds for a meal along the way. You can find them on the table near the candle, my child."

The novice took a flaxen bag hanging on the wall and placed the wrapped rice and package of sesame salt inside. The Noble Teacher waited outside for Amazing Jewel and the novice, and then lightly closed the door. They went around to the back of the hermitage and began to climb a slope. The climbing was very steep in some places. The Noble Teacher carried a staff of bamboo. Despite the hard going, Amazing Jewel could see that her father could still climb nimbly on legs that appeared hardy. For ten years he had refused to be carried uphill or downhill in a sedan chair. No doubt by now he was completely accustomed to climbing steep mountain paths. The novice was an expert climber, too. He stopped frequently to wait for Amazing Jewel, offering his hand to prevent her from slipping. When they arrived at the hermitage, called Dauntlessness, Amazing Jewel was aware of the fragrant scent of flowers wafting in the breeze. It was the perfume of magnolia, so familiar to her. As a child, she used to pick magnolia flowers to put in her hair whenever she visited Self-Blessed Temple near the palace. Many magnolia trees were flowering in front of the little Dauntlessness Hermitage.

"Dharma Lamp," she called out to the novice, "look at all the magnolia flowers!"

Dharma Lamp responded, "All of these magnolia trees were planted by the Noble Teacher, Sister, when I was only three years old!" The trees towered over their heads.

They followed the Noble Teacher around the left side of the hermitage. Here the novice pointed out two other hermitages, one called Mortar and the other Medicine. He explained how in former times the royal physicians came here to gather herbs and refine them into medicine. Mortar Hermitage was where they ground the herbs, and Medicine Hermitage was where they dispensed the herb pills. Amazing Jewel knew that these medicines were used for the royal family and also distributed to the people in times of epidemic and famine. The famous Jewel of Dew pills were made in this very place. In years of drought, temples were entrusted with the distribution of rice to the hungry, and families with sick members were given Jewel of Dew pills. Amazing Jewel entered Medicine Hermitage and found it quite spacious. Inside were many wooden drawers used to store medicinal herbs.

The Noble Teacher led them on a well-worn path towards Violet Clouds Hermitage. After a good climb, he suggested they rest in a rocky spot where clusters of bamboo grew between the stones. Dharma Lamp took out the rice and sesame salt and offered some to the Noble Teacher, who sat on a stone slab in the lotus position. The monk said grace and accepted the rice, chewing slowly to enjoy every bite. Dharma Lamp then handed some rice to Amazing Jewel before serving himself. He, too, said a silent grace before eating. When the meal was over, the novice picked a leaf and folded it into a cone. He ran to the nearby stream. Amazing Jewel followed him. He filled the leaf cup with water for the Noble Teacher. Amazing Jewel knelt on a large stone and scooped up a handful of the cool, refreshing water.

She watched the crystal clear stream tumble over the rocks. Her mind was unusually serene, without a trace of unsettling anxiety or desire. She was almost at the uppermost summit of Mount Yen Tu, near the person she loved and respected most. He was her father, but he was also the person who understood her better than anyone else. She wondered how many people truly understood the Noble Teacher's heart. Though she had not yet read all his books, such as *Words from the Stone Cave*, *The Truly Meditative Mind: A Record*, *Records of the Bamboo Forest*, or *Collected Poems*, she knew that few people, even those who had read all of these, understood him as well as she did.

Amazing Jewel suddenly turned her attention to the novice. He, too, had scooped up a handful of water, and now sat along the stream bank, playfully dabbling at the water. The sight of his two hands made her heart jump. When she was the same age as Dharma Lamp, she, too, loved to dabble her hands in water. Back then she never really stopped to look at her hands as she had two years earlier at her father's beckoning. That day, her father had opened her eyes. Now, she looked at the novice's hands, and felt she could truly see them. Although they were Dharma Lamp's hands, he had probably never seen them as clearly as she did now. Dharma Lamp was the Noble Teacher's spiritual son, but she guessed that her father had not yet opened his eyes in a way which would allow him to see the true nature of his hands. He had been a novice for two years, living in a world of purity, joy, and peace, although he did not fully realize it. His thoughts were bent on the future. He wanted to study hard to become an eminent monk like Phap Loa, sitting on a dais before the admiring eyes of the King, ministers, and people. Amazing Jewel knew that the novice still had a long path to tread, and affection welled in her heart. She understood that the long path was not his alone, for she was now aware that she and the novice were not truly separate from one another.

Looking at the novice's hands, Amazing Jewel's thoughts turned to her son, Dayada. She experienced a compassion which did not come from her alone, but seemed to spring from her father's heart, as well. Here were her hands that she had also transmitted to her child. Who would he transmit them to in the future? And what about the hands of the novice? Her father loved Dharma Lamp. Although the novice's hands did not share his teacher's same blood, they were no different from the Noble Teacher's hands, or her own. After only a day of acquaintance, Amazing Jewel felt the same love for Dharma Lamp as she did for her brothers. Amazing Jewel suddenly saw how her life had already entered a new direction. Her heart, like her hands, was journeying into the future with no possibility of turning back. She wanted to share these new feelings with her father. She would ask him to guide her on the path that led to her own true nature.

"Let us continue, my children," said the Noble Teacher. Startled from her thoughts, Amazing Jewel saw that the Noble Teacher was standing, as was the novice. Dharma Lamp flung the flaxen bag, now empty, over one shoulder. They followed the well-worn path in single file, the Noble Teacher leading and Dharma Lamp behind. Although it was steep, it was not a difficult climb. Amazing Jewel noticed many lovely bushes of bamboo. From time to time she stopped to listen to the babbling stream. At last they reached Violet Clouds.

It was strange to see clouds floating beneath her as she stood before the hermitage. The novice pointed out Mount Dong Cuu in the distance, and, looking to the right, she could see the Southern Ocean. Its curving straits looked like an oyster shell. This was paradise. She felt she had left the worldly life of her past forever behind.

The Noble Teacher said to the novice, "Master Bao is away. Why don't you sweep out the hermitage and then make some tea." He turned to Amazing Jewel and said, "Now I am going to take you to the very top of the mountain."

He led her behind the hermitage to another well-worn path. They came to a pass where a thick grove of flowering bamboos grew. The Noble Teacher told her that this place was called Bamboo Flower Pass. They proceeded on up to the mountain's summit, which was covered with a wide expanse of bamboo jutting from among rocks. Amazing Jewel found the intermingling of bamboo and rock most pleasing. There were also two lotus ponds. The flowers had already withered, leaving only seed pods floating on the water's surface.

Amazing Jewel followed her father until they came to a square, smooth slab of rock at the very top of the mountain and there they sat down. Sitting on the highest peak of Mount Yen Tu with her beloved father, Amazing Jewel felt as though she had climbed to heaven. There was, in fact, a legend that gods flew down to this spot from time to time to play chess and drink wine. She

*The Noble Teacher spoke little, but Amazing Jewel had only
to look into his kind eyes to know how happy he was.*

imagined this slab of stone to be the very table on which they played.

The Noble Teacher spoke little, but Amazing Jewel had only to look into his kind eyes to know how happy he was. As yet, no hermitage had been built here, but she guessed the Noble Teacher often visited this spot. No doubt, he himself had planted the lotus in the ponds. Amazing Jewel stood up and looked in all directions. The blue sky was immense, and far below stretched the ocean. She knew that on a cloudy day, she would not be able to see anything, neither sky nor sea. The capital lay far to the west. There, her eldest brother held court and ruled over the kingdom. But it was the Buddhist teacher, seated here on this slab, whom the people loved the most. In former times, he repelled the Mongol invaders and protected the borders. He had been willing to part with his own daughter to bring reconciliation between Viet and Cham. Here on the mountain, with no royal throne, no citadel, no soldiers, only tiny, thatched huts, dwelled the very heart of the country, the heart of the Way. Amazing Jewel looked at her father, filled with admiration.

He turned, smiled gently at her, and said, "I wanted you to meet Master Bao Sat, your elder brother in the Dharma, but you will have to wait a few more days. I sent him to the capital on a small errand this morning." Bao Sat was delivering an urgent message to King Anh Tong from the Noble Teacher, asking that 300 highly skilled Champa craftsmen working in the capital be allowed to return to their homeland as an indirect apology for the kidnapping of Amazing Jewel. "Master Bao Sat will reach the capital tomorrow. I told him to tell the King that he must not regret losing the craftsmen, no matter how skilled they are. I suggested the court arrange for them to return by ship and that a landowner of Hoa district act as their guide. I hope that by this action, Champa feelings of indignation will be softened."

Amazing Jewel was moved. Even though he sat atop a lofty mountain, her father continued to find ways to serve the common good. How was it this silent monk understood the life of the world so profoundly? Amazing Jewel did not need to speak her thoughts. She knew her father had seen into her heart's deepest feelings. No doubt he also saw the peace and joy awakened in her since that very morning. A teardrop formed and clung to her eyelash, glistening like a pearl. A long moment passed before the tear gathered enough weight to fall. Amazing Jewel smiled gently. Perhaps this was the first human tear ever to fall on the gods' stone table. But it was not a tear of sorrow, it was a tear of joy.

CHAPTER SEVEN

PEARL

Tiger Mountain Village, *1312*

After a day and night of travel, the boat docked in Vu Xa, and Pearl, carrying a bag, disembarked with the other passengers. She marveled she had somehow managed to sleep while sitting in the hold with everyone else. Pearl was determined to begin the morning-long walk to Tiger Mountain Village without delay. She hoped to reach Young Mountain Convent before the heat of midday. Once there, she could rest beneath the cool shade of the trees. Just thinking about the sweet fragrance of the flowering trees in the convent courtyard gave her a rush of energy.

She had lost count of her many visits to the convent to visit Sister Fragrant Garland. Every visit required at least three days. The journey there was quick enough, but the return trip against the river's current was arduous and slow. This time she had requested five days' leave from Lord Van Hue Vuong, in whose household she worked. After all, it was the feast of the Buddha's nativity.

The market was already being set up as the boat docked, though vendors still outnumbered customers. Pearl crossed the marketplace and followed the road which led through the village, passing people on their way to market. When she came to the end of the village, she turned to follow a path through the rice fields. The rice plants, a variety from Cham, were a delicate, tender green. She breathed in the sweet fragrance of the rice paddy and the early morning. Feeling restored, she walked quickly, now and again transferring the bag to her other shoulder. Because she knew the road well, she could proceed without tarrying.

In her bag she carried two small blocks of Chinese ink, one imperial jackdaw brush, and fourteen regular brushes, 500 sheets of paper, and some cakes and fruit she had bought the day before. Ink, paper, and brushes were for the nun, Sister Fragrant Garland, while the vegetarian cakes and fruit were to offer the convent. Many vegetarian cakes were being made and sold in the capital for the Buddha's nativity. Sister Fragrant Garland had asked her to buy a small amount of paper when she next visited the convent in order to bind notebooks for the pupils who attended the convent school. Five hundred sheets should suffice for now. The day before boarding the boat, Pearl stopped at Khanh's bookstore and Khanh donated the paper as a gift to Young Mountain Convent. The ink and brushes were a personal gift from her to Sister Fragrant Garland. Khanh, also Princess Amazing Jewel's former attendant, was now married and therefore could not leave home as easily as Pearl to visit the nun, their former mistress.

I hope Khanh's husband will have better luck with the exam this year, thought Pearl. Khanh had been married four years. She had opened the paper shop to help support her husband, a student. A year after they were wed, Khanh gave birth to a baby girl, and the young couple brought the baby to meet Sister Fragrant Garland. Every time she went to visit their former mistress, Pearl stopped by Khanh's bookshop to invite her to come along, but Khanh was always too busy.

Pearl looked down at the clothes and the pair of clogs she was wearing. No doubt, she would be scolded by Sister Fragrant Garland for not dressing more simply when she visited the convent. This dress and these clogs were the simplest things she owned, but having come this far, she realized they were not as simple as she would have liked. It was difficult for her to dress like a country girl. She had been a palace attendant since she was seventeen. After returning from Cham, she served as a lady-in-waiting to the Queen, and then went to serve in the household of Lord Van Hue Vuong, on Amazing Jewel's recommendation.

He was a renowned literary scholar whose magnanimous heart matched his extensive learning. He promised Amazing Jewel that he would look on Pearl as his own daughter and would be responsible for finding her a suitable husband.

Princess Amazing Jewel was ordained a nun and was given the name Sister Fragrant Garland on New Year's Day 1309, just three months after returning from Cham. Pearl had also wanted to become a nun and to remain by the Princess' side, but Amazing Jewel would not hear of it. She told Pearl that people become ordained to strive to liberate themselves and others, not just to be near someone else. But while she strongly advised Pearl not to seek ordination, she certainly could not forbid it. "You can be ordained if you insist, but I will not allow you to live in the same convent as me. People take monastic orders in order to transcend the ties of the world, not to wait on someone else like a servant, even if they feel respect and affection for that person."

Pearl did not consider herself astute, but she knew the nun was right. She had served the Princess from the age of twelve and had grown accustomed to feeling that the Princess' happiness was her own. If something made the Princess anxious, she felt anxious. When the Princess had asked Pearl to accompany her to Cham, Pearl was beside herself with joy. When Khanh returned home to marry, Pearl was content to remain in Cham. She was ready to take a Champa husband if it allowed her to stay near the Princess. Pearl remembered how angry the Princess became when she begged to be allowed to mount the funeral pyre with her. It was the first time she had ever been so severely scolded by the Princess and it frightened her. When they returned to Viet, she believed she would stay with the Princess her whole life. Who could have guessed that only months later, Amazing Jewel would take vows? When Pearl first asked to be ordained with the Princess, Amazing Jewel said, "It would be best for you to live under the care of Lord Van Hue Vuong. I shall recommend you to him. He is a man of great kindness. Then you should think about taking a husband. Becoming a nun is not right for everyone."

Pearl remembered how when the Princess returned from visiting her father on Mount Yen Tu, she refused to let Pearl call her "My Lady" anymore. She asked Pearl to call her "Sister," just as she had told the novice Dharma Lamp. At first Pearl could not bring herself to do this, and it took an entire month before she was able to address the Princess as "Sister." She never would have guessed that one word could be so difficult to pronounce!

This visit, Pearl had important news. She was to be married the following November. Lord Van Hue had arranged for her to marry a young scholar from the north named Mr. Sinh. Pearl had met him briefly when he visited the Lord's house. Lord Van Hue said that Sinh showed great promise. Since Pearl had lost both her parents at a young age, the Lord assumed the role of her father. He had already received the betrothal gifts from Sinh's family that February.

Whenever Pearl visited Young Mountain Convent, Sister Fragrant Garland was happy to hear news of the current political situation and everyone's health, but not any court intrigues or gossip. By nature Pearl was quite talkative, and so she liked to visit Khanh's shop. Khanh could listen for hours and never get bored.

Pearl didn't understand why since the day the Princess returned to Viet, her appearance had changed. She looked younger and more at ease. Though Amazing Jewel had loved her life in Cham, and had often conversed happily there, the atmosphere in the palace was, on the whole, solemn and anxious. When the Princess first returned from visiting the sacred places on Mount Yen Tu with her father, Pearl found her as carefree and cheerful as a child. It was as though she had been reborn, as though the Noble Teacher had performed some kind of magic that made it possible for the Princess to begin anew. Not long ago, Amazing Jewel had been a pampered young princess living a sheltered life in the palace. Now she was a mature woman and, at the same time, more gentle and open-hearted. Whenever Pearl mentioned King Harijit or Prince Dayada, the Princess no longer wept in grief. It was not because she wanted to forget her husband and her son—indeed, she missed them both—yet Pearl noticed a special quality in the Princess' voice that seemed to express a recognition that the King and Prince were still very much with her.

———

Pearl had never seen the Princess so grief-stricken as the day they received news that the Noble Teacher had departed this life at his Sleeping Clouds Hermitage on Mount Yen Tu. Pearl remembered the date well. It was the third day of the eleventh month in 1308. The Noble Teacher entered *mahaparinirvana* at midnight of the first day of the eleventh month. At midday on the following day, the temple in the capital received the sad news and a temple messenger was sent to inform King Anh Tong. At that time, Pearl was staying in Self-Blessed Temple on the palace grounds. King Anh Tong summoned his sister, and when she heard the news, Amazing Jewel shut herself in her room for an entire day and night. Pearl was surprised that the Princess did not want to go to Mount Yen Tu to attend her father's funeral, even though King Anh Tong had sent a messenger to invite her.

The entire country was plunged into grief. The people felt as though they had been orphaned. Pearl herself was unable to attend the funeral rites on the mountain but was told that thousands did. For fifteen consecutive days and nights, bells of mourning were rung in every temple. The Princess knelt all day at Self-Blessed Temple until the vessel containing the Noble Teacher's relics was brought there from Mount Yen Tu.

Within a month, the Princess became a nun. She was ordained in the Strength of Tranquility Temple by Bao Phac, the National Buddhist Teacher, who transmitted the precepts to her and gave her the name "Fragrant Garland." The National Teacher was one of the foremost disciples of the Noble Teacher. The day after she received the precepts, Sister Fragrant Garland joined the community of the Strength of Tranquility Temple to pursue her study of the Way together with a number of other young nuns, taught by the National Teacher himself. In the tenth month, he entrusted Sister Fragrant Garland with responsibility for Tiger Mountain Convent in the province of Nam Dinh. The convent was situated on a rocky mountain. When she wanted to visit, Pearl had to travel by boat down Nhi Ha River to Vu Xa from where she proceeded by foot.

The first time she visited Tiger Mountain, Pearl was met by a nine-year-old girl named Dawn at the foot of the mountain, and then led up to the convent. Dawn, the daughter of Mr. Truc who plowed the convent's rice field, lived at the foot of the mountain and attended the convent school every day. While Pearl waited in the guest room, Dawn went to let Sister Fragrant Garland know a visitor had arrived. Pearl could hear Sister Fragrant Garland ask, "Who is our visitor?" and the child's reply, "I don't know, Sister, but she is wearing a very fancy gown." Pearl could not help smiling. That day she had indeed worn an elegant dress. No one in the countryside dressed like that. Sister Fragrant Garland was overjoyed to see that the guest was Pearl.

They talked until it was time for the afternoon service. Then Pearl followed the nun to the shrine room and met the other three nuns who lived at the convent. The eldest, Still Radiance, was forty years old. She had been asked by Sister Fragrant Garland to take the position of Abbess. Although Sister Fragrant Garland was just twenty-two, the other two nuns were even younger— Sister Peace Blossom was twenty-one, and Sister Fragrant Glory was seventeen. Like Sister Fragrant Garland, they had both studied the Buddhadharma under the National Teacher on Mount Tranquility.

That first night, Pearl slept in the convent. Sister Fragrant Garland suggested Pearl wear something simpler the next time she visited. After all, Young Mountain Convent was a modest, rural convent. Pearl looked at the way she was dressed and then at the nun. Who could ever have guessed that the young nun had been both a princess and a queen? The nun's dark brown robe was woven from a coarse flax material. She wore reed sandals in the shrine room, but outside went barefoot. Sister Fragrant Garland had learned to use a hoe. She could weed, sow, spread manure, and care for the nursery garden. Her young pupil, Dawn, had shown her how to do many of these things. Taking the nun's hands into her own, Pearl noticed they were no longer soft like her own. They were the hands of someone accustomed to working in the garden and rice field, roughened by calluses. Sister Fragrant Garland covered her head with a brown scarf like the other nuns, and although her face was still fresh and bright, she had undergone a remarkable change. The marks of royalty had utterly vanished. Unadorned as a palm tree, she reminded Pearl of a young, green banana leaf. Although there was a great deal of work for the nuns to share, Pearl was struck by how relaxed Sister Fragrant Garland appeared. She was always smiling. The nun frequently referred to words spoken by the Noble Teacher: "The unbusied heart is free to do all it wants. There is no other meditation teaching than this." It was difficult for Pearl to understand. How could someone with as much work as Sister Fragrant Garland still have time to show concern for so many others, such as the sick children in the village below?

Pearl learned that the convent owned three acres of rice fields which were just enough to supply the needs of the convent and Mr. Truc's family. Yet when the Queen, Bao Tu, expressed her intention to offer twenty-five acres of fertile land to the convent, Sister Fragrant Garland refused. And when Prince Hue offered the convent ten acres, she refused as well. Even when the district governor wanted to offer five acres, Sister Fragrant Garland refused. These offers caused some disagreement in the convent. The nun who oversaw the running of Young Mountain Convent, Sister Still Radiance, discussed the matter at length with Sister Fragrant Glory. She believed that by increasing its acreage, the convent could become a practice center that would attract many students. The nuns would then be relieved of some of their hard work. But Sister Fragrant Garland thought differently. At first Pearl, too, failed to understand why Sister Fragrant Garland would turn down such generous gifts. Earlier that year, Queen Bao Tu had given 500 acres to Bao An Temple. With the support provided by many rice fields, the monks had the time and means to take in many students and to perform good works, as well. Pearl knew that the nuns at Young Mountain Convent required material support. Sister Fragrant Garland needed frequent supplies of medicine, paper, and brushes for the poor children in the village. On many occasions, she also helped support the children's parents when they were in need. With a few more acres, thought Pearl, the nuns would be able to increase their charitable work.

Pearl thought a great deal about Sister Fragrant Garland's refusal to accept the offers of land and could not arrive at any understanding. She knew the nun felt no animosity towards the Queen or Prince. On the contrary, she felt much affection for them. So why did she turn them down? After all, how much revenue could the nursery garden, on which the nun lavished such care, bring in?

Sister Fragrant Garland planted many varieties of plants including cypress, rhododendron, peony, and magnolia. The nuns spent hours splitting bamboo to make baskets the size of large pumpkins to pot the young plants. Pine trees, for example, about eighteen inches high, were uprooted together with a ball of earth and planted in the bamboo baskets. Twice a month in the autumn, Mr. Truc and little Dawn carried the trees by boat to sell in the capital. Nobility often bought these trees to plant in their own gardens. All the temples in the area loved to plant varieties of pine, cypress, and magnolia. Many benefactors came to buy plants directly from the convent nursery to make offerings at other temples. Sister Fragrant Garland put great effort into caring for the convent's nursery. She seemed to treasure every leaf and every branch, attending to each plant as if it were a prince without peer. Pearl knew the market district where Mr. Truc took the plants to sell, and she introduced many acquaintances to the plants there.

From the day Sister Fragrant Garland went to live at Young Mountain Convent, she ceased all direct contact with people in the capital. Pearl must have been the only convent benefactor who came from as far away as the capital, but Pearl never had much money or other gifts to offer. She managed to visit only every three or four months, and then brought only a modest amount of paper, ink, candles, sandalwood, and fruit. Sister Fragrant Garland never accepted offerings from the royal family, but happily accepted whatever Pearl brought. This gladdened Pearl and made her feel as close to the Princess as she had in former years.

Only one thing caused her chagrin, and that was when people told her things she dared not share with Sister Fragrant Garland. Once Lord Van Hue Vuong asked Pearl about their perilous journey from Cham back to the Viet capital. Pearl recounted the journey in detail, from the time the Princess' boat left shore to perform the ceremony for the late King Harijit, to when their boat was forced to shore for repairs after being caught in a storm, to the time they spent in hiding while waiting for the ill-fated capture of Prince Dayada. Lord Van Hue Vuong drew a long breath and said he regretted that the malicious gossip of a few had so embroidered the story that it sounded as though the Princess had been having an affair with the minister in charge of the kidnap operation. Pearl was very annoyed. Why would anyone spread such a story? The ministers and seamen aboard knew perfectly well that nothing of the sort had taken place. Lord Van Hue Vuong instructed Pearl not to relate such harmful gossip to Sister Fragrant Garland, and Pearl obeyed. He went on to tell her many other annoying things. For example, when the Princess left to live in Cham, there were members of the court who were displeased and said such things as, "Why take branches of gold and leaves of pearl from the capital to offer to a bunch of jungle savages?"

They made songs to mock the marriage whose lyrics said such things as, "What a shame to transplant a cinnamon tree in the jungle for the rascal Harijit to climb!" Another song intended to slander the Princess and minister said, "What a shame to wash your pure white grains of rice in muddy water and cook them over a fire of straw!" When people say such things, they are like the frog who sits at the bottom of the well, thinking the lid to his well is the sky, thought Pearl. How dare people call Cham a land of savages when Cham possesses so fine a civilization and so talented a King? Their attitude was no different from the scorn heaped on Viet by the Mongolian dynasty.

Nobody knows my lady better than I, thought Pearl. No noble had touched Amazing Jewel, let alone the minister in charge of the kidnapping operation. Such rumors made Pearl livid. She also knew that Lord Van Hue Vuong was right. She shouldn't sully the ears of the Princess with such stories.

The head of Tiger Mountain village hired a teacher for the village children—these were twenty-one pupils from age seven to fourteen. These children came from well-off families who could afford school supplies. Sister Fragrant Garland, along with Sisters Peace Blossom and Fragrant Glory, taught a small class of poor children at the convent. Sister Fragrant Garland had visited their homes to persuade their parents to allow them to attend the convent school. Lessons lasted two hours every afternoon, with a holiday on every full moon, new moon, and religious festival. Sister Fragrant Garland helped the parents understand that all children needed an education to prevent them from being easily deceived in life by others. There were seven girls and nine boys; Dawn was the eldest girl. Some boys who tended water buffalo for rich families did not return home until after dark, and the nuns had not yet found a way to provide them with schooling. The poor children who were able to come were very happy for the chance. They studied the texts *Three Words to a Sentence*, *Poetry of Five Words to a Line*, and *Questions for Beginners*. They also read *The Teachings of the Buddha*. Most of these books Pearl had bought or requested from Khanh's shop. The 500 sheets of

*Sister Fragrant Garland…taught
a small class of children at the convent.*

paper Pearl carried in her bag would be made into exercise books for the children to learn to write.

Pearl's thoughts were interrupted when she suddenly realized she had already reached the district market. It was crowded with shoppers, and Pearl joined the throng. She put down her bag and reached for money to buy some sesame candy, steamed dumplings, and baked cakes. She asked the stall-holder to wrap them carefully in a dried banana leaf, and then she placed them gently in her bag. She left the marketplace and walked in the direction of the bridge. It was not far from here to Tiger Mountain village. This time Pearl would be able to stay at the convent three days. It would probably be the last time she visited her former mistress before she married. The marriage, after all, was only six months away.

Pearl intended to share the news of her wedding in private with Sister Fragrant Garland. If the other nuns found out, she would feel embarrassed. Pearl, now twenty-three, remembered how she had so stubbornly insisted on being ordained a nun along with the Princess. Now she could see how right Sister Fragrant Garland had been. Since early spring, a day didn't pass without her imagining what it would be like to have a husband and a family. She couldn't keep such thoughts away. How strange! She did not know Mr. Sinh, yet after only one brief meeting, she could not forget the image of his face. People spoke of the happy fate that brings people together, and Pearl felt that it had happened for her. What if Sister Fragrant Garland had allowed her to be ordained? In seeing her own heart more clearly, Pearl felt most grateful to the nun. She hoped that after she left to go live with her husband, she would be allowed to visit Sister Fragrant Garland from time to time. Perhaps her husband would even join her. She would love to introduce Mr. Sinh to Sister Fragrant Garland.

Pearl arrived at the foot of Tiger Mountain. She shifted her bag to her other shoulder and hastened her steps. The sun blazed down as the convent bell rang out. Midday hours in the country were uncannily still. Pearl guessed that the nuns were chanting the midday office and making offerings. Yes, she was right. She could hear the sound of the wooden drum intermingled with chanting.

She stopped by the Trucs' house. Mrs. Truc, Dawn's mother, was overjoyed to see her.

"Miss Pearl, how wonderful to see you! Have you come on a visit?"

On making inquiries, Pearl learned that Mr. Truc was still working in the rice field and Dawn was up at the convent. Mrs. Truc went outside. She opened an earthernware jar and, using a coconut shell, ladled out a cup of water for Pearl. Pearl thanked her and relished the rainwater down to the last drop. It was so refreshing! She turned the cup upside down and said to Mrs. Truc, "Later in the day, I shall come down from the convent to visit with you and Mr. Truc."

Mrs. Truc nodded her head in agreement. "Yes, yes. This afternoon we'd love to have you visit. My husband will be very happy to see you."

Pearl took up her bag and walked out the gate. She turned to her left and took a shortcut up the mountain. She frequently stopped to rest in the cool shade of trees. When she arrived at the convent, she saw several children clustered in the courtyard beside the meditation hall. Catching sight of Dawn among them, she crossed the courtyard. The children were busy setting up scenery to depict the Lumbini grove for a skit about the Buddha's nativity they were to perform the next morning. Catching sight of Pearl, Dawn called out and ran up to greet her. The child's eyes sparkled. Her hair brushed against her shoulders, and she was dressed in a brown shirt and gray trousers.

"Miss Pearl! Miss Pearl!" Dawn took hold of Pearl's arm. She took Pearl's bag and placed it on the stone step and then gazed affectionately at Pearl. Pearl stroked the child's hair and asked, "Is Sister Fragrant Garland busy in the convent, my child?"

"Sister isn't in the convent, Miss. She went down to the village this morning and hasn't returned. But please come inside." Dawn slung the bag over her shoulder and waited for Pearl to enter first.

Pearl asked, "Why did Sister Fragrant Glory go down to the village? Do you know when she'll be back?"

"Sister went to visit Aunt Phung. I don't know when she will be back."

Pearl felt somewhat disappointed. She had come to the convent in hopes of spending as much time as possible with Sister Fragrant Garland. She smiled at her own impatience. Surely the nun would be back well before evening.

Entering the guest room, Pearl joined her palms in respectful greeting to Sister Still Radiance. She asked Dawn to fetch some wooden trays on which she could arrange the cakes, fruit, candy, Chinese ink, and paper. Pearl placed the trays on the table. Sister Still Radiance asked Dawn to serve Pearl some plum tea. When she learned that Pearl could stay for three days, Sister Still Radiance said, "What a lovely surprise! Sister Fragrant Garland will have an opportunity to hear all that is happening in the capital. Are you tired after your journey? Please, why don't you rest a while in one of the back rooms? Sister Fragrant Garland should be back soon. Poor Sister, she had to leave so suddenly, she didn't have time for the midday meal."

When Pearl assured the nun she did not need to rest, Sister Still Radiance said, "Let me go ask Sister Fragrant Glory to keep you company. Please excuse me, but I must finish preparing the texts for tomorrow. Fifty-two people will formally take the Three Refuges and Five Precepts. We'll have a chance to talk again this evening."

Pearl stood up and bowed to the nun. Soon afterwards, Sister Fragrant Glory, the youngest nun, entered. She smiled warmly. "Hello, Sister Pearl!"

"Hello, Sister Fragrant Glory."

"Oh, please just call me Fragrant Glory. Although I am a nun, I am younger than you!" Fragrant Glory smiled and sat down facing Pearl. She took Pearl's hands in her own.

Sister Fragrant Glory, it was true, was still very young. Pearl had known her from the time she studied Buddhism with Sister Fragrant Garland at Strength of Tranquility Temple. Sister Fragrant Garland was very fond of Sister Fragrant Glory. Seeing that the young nun possessed both wisdom and goodness, she asked her to take up residence at Young Mountain Convent when they finished their studies together.

"Sister Fragrant Garland is finding a doctor for Aunt Phung. She is having difficulty with her pregnancy. The time for her delivery is quite near and there is no one at home to help her. Her husband was killed in a war expedition to Cham last year, and so mother and son are all alone." Phung's son was named Loi. He was the same age as Dawn and also a pupil at Young Mountain Convent.

Suddenly Fragrant Glory noticed the paper and brushes arranged on the tray. Delighted, she said, "You have brought us paper and ink! Wonderful! Now there will be a present for each of the children on the Buddha's nativity. I will stay up tonight and bind exercise books for each child."

A flurry of conversation drifted in from the courtyard. Pearl looked out and saw a group of women, four older and three younger, carrying baskets on their heads and shoulders. The baskets were filled with rice, beans, vegetables, and fruit, and they put them down in front of the storeroom as offerings for the vegetarian feast for the Buddha's nativity. On the feast of the nativity, every temple in the land cooked a vegetarian meal to offer anyone who came. On that day nobody need fear going hungry, including roadside beggars dressed in rags. Everyone who came to the temple was welcomed with open arms. The food was shared with nobility and poor alike. It was such a lovely custom, she mused. She decided she must enter the kitchen later to see what kinds of vegetarian dishes were cooked in this region. She ate vegetarian meals quite often at the home of Lord Van Hue Vuong, but no doubt people here in the countryside prepared different kinds of dishes.

A moment later another group of people arrived at the convent carrying birds in cages and fish in large earthernware jars. Pearl knew that these were the birds and fish to be released on the Buddha's nativity. After the morning ceremony of bathing a statue of the newly-born Buddha, the nuns would open the cages and let the birds fly free. In the afternoon, the fish would be released into the river. Crowds of people would gather along the shore. When prayers had been said and the fish released, everyone would light a candle to set afloat on the water. Thousands of flickering candle-boats would be carried on the currents. This was called the "Ceremony of Releasing the Light." Pearl had attended many such ceremonies in the capital, but this would be the first time she had an opportunity to see one in the countryside.

CHAPTER EIGHT

FRAGRANT GLORY

It was already late at night. Laughter and talking no longer drift-ed from the kitchen, so Pearl guessed that everyone else had gone to bed. Sister Fragrant Glory rested her hands. All day she had been working in the kitchen—putting beans to soak, chop-ping vegetables, laying out bowls. Tomorrow was the Buddha's birthday, and cooking a vegetarian meal for everyone who might come to the convent the next day was a large undertaking. Fra-grant Glory smiled sweetly as she sat in her room binding the children's exercise books by the light of a peanut-oil lamp. She thought about the caged birds. They would be released when the sun rose high in the sky tomorrow. She thought about the fish and how she had poured fresh water into their earthernware jars. They would be released at dusk. One jar was filled with baby fish, and she wondered if any of them would be captured and then released again at the Buddha's nativity next year. Before the birds and fish were given their freedom, they received the Three Ref-uges. This year Young Mountain Convent would liberate twelve cages of birds and five large jars of fish—200 birds and 3,000 fish in all.

People often bought baby fish for the releasing ceremony as it was possible to buy many and thus save more lives. Fragrant Glory thought of the total number of fish that would be set free throughout Viet. A temple could always be found, no matter where one travelled. Every village had one and some had two. Tomorrow so many birds would return to the sky and so many fish to the water. It was a happy thought. Lord Buddha had passed into mahaparinirvana nearly 2,000 years ago, but thanks to his goodness, countless living beings continued to be released from suffering. "Homage to Avalokitesvara, the Bodhisattva of Compassion!" murmured Fragrant Glory. "Tomorrow no one will go hungry. Everyone will have a vegetarian meal, and no ox, hen, or pig needs to be killed either!" Silently, Fragrant Glory thanked the Buddha. Tears filled her eyes. Every year there was one day like this, a day of no killing, a day of no hatred, a day on which no one would go to bed hungry. If only all the days of the year were like the Buddha's nativity, how much happiness there would be for all beings.

As she continued to bind the exercise books, Fragrant Glory thought about the day. That afternoon she had not held class but instead helped the children hang up flowers and lanterns all around the convent. She also helped them rehearse their skit about the Buddha's birth. Dawn played the part of Queen Maya, the mother of the Buddha. She wore a piece of yellow cloth, a remnant of one of Sister Fragrant Glory's robes. Thom and Uyen played Maya's two attendants. Loi was to have played the part of the wise Master Asita, but because his mother was ill, Thong was asked to take his place. Thong fashioned a funny fake beard from a banana leaf to attach to his chin, but he did not make as convincing an Asita as Loi, who could imitate an old man's hoarse voice perfectly.

The convent school was Sister Fragrant Glory's favorite work. Because the children all came from poor homes, they spent mornings helping their parents with chores, and then came up to the convent in the early afternoon. In the late afternoon, they returned home to help out with more work. They were all well-behaved and easy to teach. Dawn wanted to become a nun like her teachers. She had been granted permission to live at the convent as a novice, but Sister Fragrant Garland said she should wait until she was sixteen or seventeen years old before making the decision whether to be ordained as a nun. She was bright and quick, easily the best pupil in class. She also studied the liturgy and could now follow the evening office. Dawn reminded Sister Fragrant Glory of herself as a child.

Fragrant Glory was the youngest child of a school teacher from Lo Long Hung district. Her mother died when she was only ten. Her elder brother was a monk at the monastery in Tien Lu. She wanted very much to follow in his footsteps but had to wait until she was sixteen before her father would give his permission. She became a novice at Strength of Tranquility Temple and was a student of the National Meditation Teacher, Bao Phac, along with Sister Fragrant Garland. As they shared their studies, Fragrant Glory grew to love and respect Sister Fragrant Garland. When Sister Fragrant Garland was appointed abbess of Young Mountain Convent, Fragrant Glory expressed her wish to accompany her, and Master Bao Phac granted her request.

Even though Fragrant Glory knew that Sister Fragrant Garland had been a nun only four years, she looked on her as a great teacher. She also knew that Sister Fragrant Garland was once a princess but felt no distance between herself and Sister Fragrant Garland, who lived more simply than any other nun she knew. She even insisted that Sister Still Radiance take the position of abbess, not she. Fragrant Glory had met many nuns at Strength of Tranquility Temple, some practitioners for more than twenty years, but none were as simple and unassuming as Sister Fragrant Garland.

Some women become nuns because they are unhappy with their lives, others in order to take refuge in the Buddha. It was clear that Sister Fragrant Garland took vows because she wanted to lead a simple life, filled with peace and joy. Fragrant Glory considered herself lucky to be able to practice alongside Sister Fragrant Garland. She had learned so much from her in the past two years. If she only wanted to increase her knowledge of Buddhist studies, she could study at any convent. But the way to learn from Sister Fragrant Garland was to live beside her. She knew many nuns who had studied the Buddhist code of ethics in great detail, but they didn't radiate the open, free, and tolerant spirit of Buddhism as did Sister Fragrant Garland. Many nuns were overly austere and lacked the freshness of "beginner's mind."

Sister Fragrant Garland taught that liberation was found in how you lived your daily life and not something you hoped for in the future. If you couldn't experience liberation in the present moment, you would never experience it. It was clear to Fragrant Glory that Sister Fragrant Garland lived a liberated life and was able to do so because she had untied the ropes of affliction that usually bind one's heart and mind. Sister Fragrant Garland's words were simple and easy to understand, unlike many sutra commentaries. Sister Fragrant Garland told her about the peace and joy she experienced upon hearing Dharma Lamp's chanting one early morning at Little Dragon Hermitage. Fragrant Glory understood then that her elder sister had undergone the experience described in Buddhist meditation as "dying to be reborn." Because of that, she could taste such bliss. Sister Fragrant Garland had been prepared to mount the funeral pyre and have her body burned to ashes. Springing from a deep acceptance of her death was the ability to begin a wholly new life. For the first time in her twenty-one years, she understood the peace and joy that arise when we put an end to all longing. From that point on, Sister Fragrant Garland was determined not to lose even one moment of her life. She found peace and joy in the heart of everyday tasks like threshing and hulling rice, spreading dung, or watering plants. Sister Fragrant Glory wanted to live like that. She knew her meditative experience still lacked the depth of Sister Fragrant Garland's but she was confident that she, too, had the capacity to achieve the same.

Although she was the daughter of a village teacher, Sister Fragrant Glory was familiar with manual work. When she went to live at Young Mountain Convent, she sought opportunities to work beside Sister Fragrant Garland. The convent had a granary and once a month they hulled rice. On full moon days and important religious holidays they made fresh tofu and pickled tofu.

Once a year they made miso. All the nuns, from the eldest to the youngest, participated in these tasks. Although Sister Fragrant Garland had spent her childhood pampered in a royal palace, with just a few months' practice she was as adept at manual labor as anyone. Sister Fragrant Garland encouraged the other nuns to practice mindful observation of the breath while hulling rice. Now whenever Fragrant Glory hulled rice, she found she was no longer distracted by the constant coming and going of her thoughts. Instead she dwelled in mindfulness, observing her breath during all her tasks—sweeping the shrine room floor, arranging flowers on the altar, washing bowls after the midday meal. Sister Fragrant Garland explained that the difference between living a worldly life and living a life of liberation was the practice of mindfulness right in the midst of one's daily work. "If we do not practice while working, how are we any different from others?" she asked. Fragrant Glory knew this was an important teaching and she was determined to apply it wholeheartedly in every moment.

By nature, Sister Fragrant Glory was quick, tidy, and efficient. She did not like tasks to be long and drawn out. When she had work to do, her main concern was to finish it as quickly as possible. Only when the task was completed, could she relax. But Sister Fragrant Garland instructed her that while she was involved in a task, she should not long for it to be over. She should be able to find joy and ease right in the task itself. One day while giving a commentary on *The Life of the Eminent Master Tue Trung*, Sister Fragrant Garland described how a monk who took great delight in patching the torn garments of his fellow monks, practiced mindfulness in the very act of sewing. One day, while mending a robe, he penetrated the unborn and undying nature of all things in the space of six stitches, realizing the six powers of Buddha himself. When she finished telling this story, Sister Fragrant Garland said, "Had the monk thought only about finishing his sewing in order to practice sitting meditation afterwards, he would not have achieved awakening during his mending."

The story made a deep impression on Sister Fragrant Glory.
From then on, whenever she felt an urge to get her work done
quickly, she returned to her breathing. She smiled in gentle compassion at her impatience and reminded herself to let her work
be her practice. How foolish I am, she would think, there is always work to be done. When this task is finished, there will always be another. If I work simply to get my tasks over with, I
will never finish!

She remembered a short poem written by a meditation teacher:

> *How wonderful!*
> *I chop wood and carry water.*
> *How wonderful!*
> *I sow corn and plant potatoes.*

In addition to the precepts at Strength of Tranquility Temple,
Fragrant Glory studied the *Surangama* and *Lankavatara Sutras*,
the *Awakening of Faith*, and the *Blue Cliff Records*. She was unable
to grasp the profound meanings contained in these commentaries. When she came to live at Young Mountain Convent, Sister
Fragrant Garland taught her the *Sutra on the Full Awareness of
Breathing (Anapanasati)*. Sister Fragrant Garland said that this was
one of the oldest sutras. When the Buddha was still alive on
Earth, his disciples practiced according to the instructions given
in this very sutra. It used simple language and was most practi-
cal in nature. It gave instruction on how to practice using the
breath in order to be aware. Sister Fragrant Garland told her that
when she was in Cham she heard monks chanting this same sutra
in Sanskrit.

Sister Fragrant Glory was proud to have an elder Dharma sister
who was so unique. Sister Fragrant Garland was one of very
few nuns who could read Sanskrit. When she recited the Three
Refuges in Sanskrit for Fragrant Glory, it sounded strange yet
wonderful.

Sister Fragrant Glory's practice had deepened recently. She had an occasion to reread the *Lankavatara Sutra* and found she could now understand sections she had not been able to penetrate before, even with great effort. She was now more centered and clear and could better focus on the details of daily life, details that continually called her back to the wonders of life. Meditation nourished her loving kindness and compassion, and she rarely criticized others as she had in the past. She was far more tolerant and able to look on others with eyes of compassion. She could better understand now how Sister Fragrant Garland could care for the village children as if each child were her own. Sister Fragrant Glory hoped to visit her father soon in order to tell him about the changes meditation had brought about in her life. She hoped he might try meditation in order to enjoy happiness and serenity in his old age.

At Young Mountain Convent, Sister Fragrant Glory was the nun closest to Sister Fragrant Garland. Perhaps it was because they were ordained by the same teacher, but it was also true that she was the most open to what Sister Fragrant Garland had to say. She was the first to understand why Sister Fragrant Garland refused to accept more land, even though the rice fields in question were being offered by the Queen. She knew that additional rice fields would complicate their life of practice. The Queen had, no doubt, offered the fields in hopes of reducing the amount of manual work the nuns had to do. But coordinating workers for the planting and harvest would, in fact, take up even more of their time, time which could be used for meditation practice. When other people offered fields as alms to the convent just to please the royal family, it was obvious why Sister Fragrant Garland refused. If local officials wished to build merit, they could do so by governing well, protecting the weak and keeping in check those who would wrong the people. They did not need to offer land to the convent. Sister Still Radiance had been upset when Sister Fragrant Garland refused to accept the Queen's offer of land, even though she agreed to go along with the community's sentiments. As for Sister Peace Blossom, she was so easygoing, there was no problem. Thus the matter of refusing the Queen's land was resolved harmoniously.

Sister Fragrant Garland had also confided in Sister Fragrant Glory about her son, Prince Dayada. "He is now barely four years old. He surely knows that his mother was the Queen Paramesvari, but has no idea what I look like. I'm sure he speaks Champa fluently, but knows not a word of Viet." When Sister Fragrant Garland mentioned her son, her eyes shone. She was in total agreement that Prince Dayada belonged to the Champa royal family, and she knew he would grow up well treated by all those around him. Reports that fighting had broken out between Cham and Viet the year before clearly distressed Sister Fragrant Garland. She wasn't only worried about her son's safety; she grieved for the loss of friendly relations between the two countries.

Sister Fragrant Glory's thoughts turned to the sad news Pearl brought concerning the war. They had spoken at dusk, before Sister Fragrant Garland returned to the convent. In Lord Van Hue Vuong's house, Pearl heard reports to which few others were privy. Exactly three years after the death of the Noble Teacher, war broke out. Although Viet waited to strike until after the period of mourning was over, war preparations had been long in the making. According to Pearl, the same minister in charge of kidnapping the Princess was the first man to propose going to war with Cham. He devised a strategy and obtained the court's consent to embark on a war expedition.

The year before, according to usual custom, the Champa ambassador to Viet was charged by King Harijitputra to bring gold, silver, and other precious objects to offer as tribute to Viet. This same ambassador was also responsible for defending Cloud Pass along the frontier Champa shared with Viet. Having first obtained King Anh Tong's consent, the Viet minister made a secret agreement with the Champa ambassador, promising the ambassador

a very high position if a Viet expedition into Cham were successful. King Anh Tong, leading the infantry, conducted the expedition himself. Prince Hue led troops up into the mountains while
another general led troops along the seacoast. In the fifth month,
the Viet army captured King Harijitputra and brought him to
Viet. His younger brother was placed on the throne in a puppet
regime. King Harijitputra was presently being guarded at a country residence in Gia Lam. Although given the title "The Loyal
Lord," in truth, he was no more than a prisoner.

Sister Fragrant Glory understood how alone Sister Fragrant
Garland must feel and how sad she would be to hear these lat-
est reports. Few people truly understood the heart of the Noble
Teacher. People could call themselves Buddhist, but few possessed the heart and eyes of compassion of the Noble Teacher and
his daughter. Virtuous behavior was often only a facade that concealed ambition and rivalry within. Such men spoke of honor and
duty. They claimed it was necessary to subjugate Harijitputra
because he could not be trusted. But how had he ever failed
to show his trust worthiness? Had any Viet been harassed near
the Champa border? The Champa always paid their tribute. The
people of Viet cursed the Sungs and Mongols for their cruelty and
aggression, so why did they act the same towards the Champa?
For whom and for what purpose did men like Loi's father give
their lives on Champa territory? How could those responsible
for the war consider themselves men of virtue? Minister Doan
Nhu Hai even paid to have a bronze bell and Buddhist statue
cast. The Nation's Teacher, Bao Phac, told Sister Fragrant
Glory that all the ministers at court took the precepts when the
Noble Teacher was still alive. When King Anh Tong requested to
receive the Eight Bodhisattva Precepts from his father, the ministers, wanting to please the King, followed by taking the Three
Refuges and Five Precepts. But, according to Bao Phac, most of
them were not really committed to practicing Buddhism. They
just followed whatever direction the wind was blowing. For

them, taking precepts was just a show. Sister Fragrant Glory knew that ceremony is not important. What is important is to live in the spirit of the precepts. When the precepts are truly part of one's life, there naturally arises true honor, which is respect for all life.

Sister Fragrant Glory also knew about the huge temple, complete with a bell tower and an imposing drum tower, built on Mount Yen Tu to commemorate the passing of the Noble Teacher. Little Dragon Hermitage became Dragon Pagoda, covered with a gleaming red-tile roof. Other temples in Viet were enlarged and embellished. Several thousand acres of rice fields were added to the lands already owned by temples. At Vinh Nghiem Pagoda alone, two or three thousand monks and nuns were ordained every year. She'd heard that Quynh Lam Pagoda now possessed 1,000 acres of rich rice fields and employed more than 1,000 workers. Bao An Temple boasted thirty-three buildings, including a shrine room, storage building, and living quarters for the monks. Two hundred new rooms had to be built to house the newly ordained monks and nuns and to provide space for study and practice.

Phap Loa, the abbot of the monastery, commissioned the casting of 1,300 bronze statues of the Buddha. Vinh Nghiem Pagoda served as the central office for the entire Buddhist congregation in Viet, and all monks and nuns were registered there. At Bao An Temple, thousands of students attended courses on the teachings of the Buddha. Interest in Buddhism had never appeared so great. Sister Still Radiance's eyes sparkled whenever she spoke of these things, and Sister Peace Blossom expressed her own joy over the expansion of Buddhist congregations. Only Sister Fragrant Garland failed to show any enthusiasm. At first Sister Fragrant Glory could not understand why. When her Dharma sister explained, she saw more clearly that large Buddhist temples and statues were not necessarily indications of a thriving practice.

When the Noble Bamboo Forest Teacher was a monk on
Mount Yen Tu, there were only ten small hermitages on the
mountain, and yet the sweet fragrance of Buddhism spread in all
directions. Throughout the country, people aspired to make a
pilgrimage to Mount Yen Tu as their spiritual home. From time
to time, the Noble Teacher came down from the mountain. Wearing his faded robe, he went among the people. He leaned on a
staff, wore reed sandals, and carried no more than a wooden bowl
in his hands. Wherever he went, people gathered to hear him
speak. He counselled the people to improve themselves by ab-
staining from wrongful actions of body, speech, and mind. There
was no one who was not moved simply by looking at the Noble
Teacher. Here was a King who had renounced all riches to live
as a simple monk. There was no one who did not trust the truth
of his words. To the north, the Mongols no longer plotted against
Viet. To the south, friendly relations were established with their
Princess enthroned as Queen of Cham. The people lived in harmony. This was a true sign of the flourishing of the Dharma. Huge
temples were not important. Although the whole court now made
offerings to monasteries and had statues and bells cast, it was
merely an outward form.

Every summer the Buddhist congregation organized monastic
retreats at the four main temples—Bao An, Sung Nghiem, Vinh
Nghiem, and Quynh Lam, as well as at the temples on Mount Yen
Tu. Every temple hosted between three and five hundred monks.
A monk who was accepted to attend the retreat at Van Yen or
Dragon Pagoda was considered to have won much merit. As a
popular folk song put it, "Anyone determined to truly taste Buddhism must go to Mount Yen Tu." The song was a reminder to
the people of the Noble Teacher and the satisfaction he found in
practicing a simple life. Sister Fragrant Glory hoped one day to
visit Van Yen Temple herself and to see the memorial stupa that
held the relics of the Noble Teacher, but she hesitated because
it had become so crowded. She confided her thoughts to Sister

Fragrant Garland, telling her how she hoped they might visit the stupa together one day, but Sister Fragrant Garland did not seem interested. She told her younger sister in the Dharma that she had already been to Mount Yen Tu. Perhaps she wanted to keep her original impression of the mountain forever imprinted in her heart, the image of a quiet Noble Teacher seated near the summit of the towering mountain peak. Sister Fragrant Glory could understand why Sister Fragrant Garland felt that way. Nonetheless, she was sad to think that one day she would have to ask permission to go to Mount Yen Tu alone in order to pay respect to the Noble Teacher's relics. She would try not to pay attention to the golden towers and precious stones of the newly-built temples. She would look instead at the clouds, pine trees, and paths winding their way up through forests that the Noble Teacher had trodden years before. If only her Dharma sister and spiritual guide would accompany her!

Although she had never had the chance to meet the Noble Teacher, she could feel his presence in his poems. She was especially fond of "Going Up Mount Bao Dai":

> *The landscape is deserted*
> *and the moss makes it seem even more ancient.*
> *It is still pale early spring.*
> *Cloud-covered mountains come close,*
> *then waver and fade.*
> *The flower-covered paths are cast with shadows.*
> *Everything is like water flowing into water.*
> *For a whole lifetime*
> *the heart always gives voice to the heart.*
> *Leaning on the magnolia,*
> *I raise a flute to my lips,*
> *as moonlight floods my heart.*

She recalled when she first entered Young Mountain Convent. When the convent was first established, it was called Tiger Mountain, but Sister Fragrant Garland changed the name. They were on a mountain, but how could it possibly compare to Mount Yen Tu? The word "young" implied something still new, something not yet developed. It expressed Sister Fragrant Garland's humility.

Sister Fragrant Glory heard that the meditation teacher Huyen Quang was the abbot of Van Yen Monastery. When he was first ordained a monk, he was a disciple of her own teacher. That made him her elder Dharma brother. She knew Huyen Quang had passed the highest examination open to court officials and served as a minister for twenty years before becoming a monk. He was renowned for his beautiful poetry written in the native nom script of Viet as well as in Chinese. His meditation students circulated one of his poems, "Van Yen Monastery." She had a copy transcribed by hand, but her knowledge of nom script was weak, and she was unable to read the whole poem.

Her lack of fluency in nom characters was largely her father's fault, since he opposed their use. He constantly told her, "If nom characters ever come into general use and replace Chinese, your father is a fool." Be that as it may, the native script was now being used extensively throughout the country. Her Dharma sister had two texts written by the Noble Teacher in nom, *Songs on the Joyful Practice Amidst the Trees and Creeks* and *Enjoying the Dharma in the Realm of Dust.*

Sister Fragrant Garland had used these two texts in her Dharma talks. Although Sister Still Radiance was the eldest and served as abbess, she never missed a session of Sister Fragrant Garland's commentaries on Buddhist texts. Everyone was aware of the depth of Sister Fragrant Garland's understanding, and wished to study with her. Sister Fragrant Glory made up her mind to devote study to nom script. Some day she would write home to her father using nom. He would have to read it. After all, nom was the writing of their own people, was it not?

Sister Fragrant Garland arrived home very late that evening, guided by two children carrying torches. Before retiring to her room, she briefly told Sister Fragrant Glory what had happened.

Loi's mother was doing better, and the terrible pain in her womb was eased. Sister Fragrant Garland had managed to summon the doctor from Y Yen. In addition, a midwife would stay by her side all night. Sister Fragrant Garland could return to the convent, her mind at rest. Before she returned, she told Loi to let her know at once if there was any worsening of his mother's condition.

Sister Fragrant Glory finished binding the last exercise book for her pupils. Outside, the air was still and calm. By now, half the night had passed. No doubt everyone else was sleeping peacefully. Buddha's nativity day would dawn soon. It would be a full day of rites and ceremonies, and she needed to get some rest herself. The wooden drum and gong would awaken the women in the convent at five o'clock in the morning, and at nine o'clock, laypeople would come to participate in the ceremony of Wesak and to pray for peace. The ceremony to initiate the birds and fish as members of the Buddhist community would be held at that time. At midday, the ceremony of bathing the baby Buddha would take place in the convent garden. People would stand closely packed in the convent courtyard. The children had thoroughly rehearsed their skit about the Buddha's birth with Sister Fragrant Garland. They would be wearing their best clothes. Under a vault of bamboo, decorated with leaves and flowers to represent a palace, Sister Fragrant Garland had placed a red clay statue of the newly-born Buddha. He stood on a lotus flower, one hand pointing to the sky above, the other to the earth below, or in their case to the water, for she had placed the statue on a rock in a small pond. An earthenware vessel containing water perfumed with herbs, leaned against the rock. Each person would join his or her palms before the baby Buddha, scoop up fragrant water in a coconut ladle, and pour it in a most respectful way over the statue of the Awakened One.

Sister Fragrant Glory placed the finished exercise books in a neat pile on her writing desk. Mindfully, she changed out of her daytime robe and then continued to follow her breathing as she lay upon her low bed. Soon she was asleep, dreaming about the

Under a vault of bamboo…Sister Fragrant Garland
had placed a red clay statue of the newly-born Buddha.

children's skit. Loi, with a banana beard, was playing the sage Asita. He leaned on a walking stick, clothed in a monk's robe. He faced King Suddhodana and Queen Maya and looked into the face of the newborn Prince. He spoke in the hoarse tones of an old priest. "Noble Sire, this Prince will become a Buddha, a Tathagata...." The sage began to weep because he knew he would not live long enough to see the Prince become a Buddha. He said something else that Sister Fragrant Glory did not hear. Her attention was fixed on the banana flower wrapped in a piece of yellow silk held by Dawn, playing the part of Queen Maya. Suddenly the banana flower stirred. A halo of brilliant light emanated from the small bundle. Looking more closely, Sister Fragrant Glory saw that the banana flower had transformed into the real infant Buddha, smiling in young Dawn's arms. Overjoyed, Sister Fragrant Glory knelt down in front of Dawn and joined her palms to pay homage.

CHAPTER NINE

A MAGIC FISH

L oi woke early and checked on his mother. She was sleeping peacefully, her breathing calm and regular, and his mind felt eased. He marveled at the medicine given his mother by the doctor from Y Yen. All day yesterday his mother had writhed in pain, but as soon as she took the bowl of herbs, she lay down peacefully and was able to sleep. Afterwards, the doctor went to spend the night at Mrs. Truc's house at the foot of the mountain. Mrs. Tu, the village midwife, was sleeping on Loi's bed, and Loi had slept on some straw spread in the middle of the room. He had expected to stay up all night looking after his mother, but after taking the medicine, she slept the night through, and Loi slept soundly, too. After a day of worry, he was worn out.

Loi went down to the kitchen. He planned to reheat the medicinal herbs infused the night before. He pulled out a wisp of straw, pushed it into the lighting stove and waited. A moment later the straw caught fire. He added more wisps of straw and blew lightly on the fire until it flared. Then he scooped away some of the ash heaped up between three blocks of stone which formed another simple stove and then transferred the burning straw into that space. He added yet more straw and then placed the fire iron on the pile of straw so it would burn more slowly. Then he placed a pan of water over the three stones, and keeping an eye on the fire to make sure it burned steadily, he took some pieces of charcoal and added them until they started to burn. Then he picked up the charcoal with tongs and put them into the first stove.

To simmer medicinal herbs, one needed a stove with a grate and some charcoal. There was only enough charcoal left to heat up his mother's medicine. Yesterday, the doctor from Y Yen told him to have enough charcoal ready to keep his mother warm at the time she gave birth. Mrs. Tu, however, said that since charcoal was too expensive, he could collect a basketful of rice husks to light the stove just as easily. She also told him to gather pieces of dried bamboo roots. When needed, Loi could light the bamboo roots and throw on the rice husks for a real blaze. She also instructed Loi to find her a piece of fresh bamboo which she split into a sharp blade in order to cut the umbilical cord.

As he was lighting the stove, Loi thought about all he had to do. First, he needed to cook some fresh rice for Mrs. Tu. There was still a pot of fish simmered in soy sauce, enough to last for days, that he could offer Mrs. Tu and his mother, but Loi remembered that everyone observed the celebration of the Buddha's birth by eating vegetarian food the entire day. He was relieved to find a jar of sesame seeds that he could roast with salt as a condiment for the rice.

The day before, Loi had been unable to bear his mother's agonized cries or the tears that flowed from her eyes. His father had been killed just three months earlier on a battlefield in Cham. If his mother died, he would be an orphan. They had no money. How could he summon a doctor? His mother urged him to find Mrs. Tu, and Mrs. Tu did everything she could to ease his mother's condition. She crushed green ginger and steeped it in wine to use as a liniment. She rubbed his mother's back with betel leaves and a handful of hair. Nothing helped. And then, miraculously, Sister Fragrant Garland appeared.

It was late afternoon. Loi was sure that Dawn told the nun he was at home caring for his ill mother. And though Sister Fragrant Garland was not a physician, her presence in the tiny hut assured Loi that everything was going to be alright. The moment the nun placed her hand on his mother's forehead, her painful cries quieted and she stopped gasping for breath. She calmed herself and answered the nun's questions about the nature of her pain. Sister Fragrant Garland showed Loi and Mrs. Tu a way to massage the woman's hands and feet, while she hurried to Y Yen to summon a doctor.

After the nun left, his mother's pains were less violent than before. Loi was sure his mother felt comforted just knowing a physician would soon be there. It was late evening before the doctor arrived, accompanied by Sister Fragrant Garland, and led by two village boys carrying torches.

The nun instructed the boys to put out the torches, and asked Loi to prepare some tea for the doctor. The man carefully felt his mother's pulse, then opened his large bag. He said that her illness had been brought on by worry and anxiety, and prescribed medicinal herbs that would serve as both a sedative and tonic. When the herbs were properly simmered, Loi's mother was propped up to drink the infusion. Then Sister Fragrant Garland helped her lie back down and covered her with a blanket.

She said, "You will feel much better now and give birth to your child without complications. Why don't you recite Avalokitesvara's name before you fall asleep? Loi will boil a second infusion of medicine for you to take in the morning."

The nun clasped Mrs. Tu's hand and gave her a few additional instructions. She asked the village boys to relight the torches and first accompany the doctor to Mrs. Truc's house, where he could spend the night, and then led her back up the mountain. Before leaving, she told Loi to summon her at once if there were any change in his mother's condition.

Loi's mother soon fell into a peaceful sleep. Relieved, Loi carried the peanut-oil lamp to the stove intending to cook some rice for Mrs. Tu, but she told him not to bother as she wasn't at all hungry. So he sat down by the stove and helped himself to some leftover rice and a bit of salted fish.

Mrs. Tu pulled up a small log and sat beside him. "Don't worry, my child. I have heard excellent things about this doctor. Your mother and the baby will surely be safe and sound. You are very fortunate! Without the good Sister's intervention, such a doctor might never have set foot in this house. Your home must have a lot of merit."

Loi couldn't help wondering about the doctor's fees. As though she could read his thoughts, Mrs. Tu said, "And don't you worry about the money. Since Sister went and fetched the doctor herself, I'm sure she intends to take care of it. In fact, I wouldn't be surprised if the doctor doesn't even ask a fee, out of respect for Sister Fragrant Garland. Now then, continue to invoke the Buddha's name and pray for your mother's health and a safe birth. But for the moment, finish your dinner! I'm going to bed. If anything happens, wake me right away."

Loi stood up and took the lamp to accompany Mrs. Tu to the upper room. But she motioned with her hand that it wasn't necessary. He sat back down and picked up another small fish with his chopsticks. He had caught every fish in the pot himself. He remembered the afternoon he sat fishing along the riverbank when Dawn came looking for him. Sister Fragrant Garland wanted him to come up to the convent for the final rehearsal of a skit about the Buddha's nativity. Loi's basket was already half full when Dawn found him. She looked into the basket and exclaimed, "How wicked you are to kill so many little fish! How can you do such a thing? They have never harmed you!"

Loi looked up at Dawn. She wore a simple brown shirt. Her black hair brushed her shoulders. Her clear, bright face reminded him of the sunshine, but her dark eyes were intense and penetrating. He didn't know how to answer. If anyone else had asked the same question, it would have been easy. He would simply have replied that people have to eat in order to live. Since ancient times, people have cultivated rice, planted vegetables, raised pigs, chickens, and fish for food. The gods gave people rice, pigs, chickens, and fish as food. That's what his mother always told him. Any adult would agree.

Loi could not answer Dawn in such a way. To him, she was like a delicate peach blossom. Such an answer would be like a violent blast of wind that scatters tender petals. Dawn was like a piece of pure white paper. Such a reply would be like spilling ink on the paper. He knew she was naive, but he had no desire to mock that naivete. He found her innocence sweet and beautiful. There was something about her that reminded him of Sister Fragrant Garland. He knew how fond the nun was of Dawn. The nun was an adult, but she, too, seemed to possess the simple innocence of a young child. That was one of the reasons he respected and loved the nun. Whenever he had a chance to sit beside Sister Fragrant Garland and talk with her, he was filled with warmth and happiness. He did not know any other adult who was so fresh and clear.

His thoughts were interrupted by a sudden tugging on his fishing pole. He lifted a tiny fish, no bigger than his toe, and took it off the hook.

Dawn said, "May I please see that fish?"

Loi hesitated before handing her the fish. She examined the wound made by the hook on its tiny mouth. She stroked the fish as if she could feel its pain.

"Poor little one! How cruel to be dragged from your water home by a sharp hook. I will set you free, little one, so please swim far away from this spot."

Loi felt as though her words were as much meant for him as for the fish. He watched Dawn release the fish. She waved her hand in the water to hasten the fish's escape and then wiped her wet hands on the corner of her blouse. She turned to Loi and said, "I need to get back to the convent. Don't forget the rehearsal. Sister Fragrant Garland is waiting for you."

After Dawn left, Loi did not catch a single fish. He wondered if the fish Dawn freed had warned all the other fish to stay away. Finally, he packed up his line and pole and carried the basket of fish home to his mother. He bathed and changed his clothes before heading up to the convent.

As he walked along, he thought about Dawn and the little fish. He was reminded of the fairy tale his mother often told about a young girl who befriended a magic fish. Grateful for the girl's kindness, the fish helped her become a queen. Dawn was like the girl in the story. Perhaps she, too, would one day become a queen. There was another strange connection, Loi realized. Sister Fragrant Garland was a princess who had become a nun. Since Dawn was so close to Sister Fragrant Garland, maybe she really would become a princess.

When Loi's father was still alive, Loi often heard his parents speak about Sister Fragrant Garland with deep respect. They said she was a princess, that she was the King's younger sister. At first, Loi found it hard to believe. A princess was supposed to live in splendor. Her clothes should be of finest silk and she should never be without attendants. A princess was carried in a fancy palanquin and escorted by royal guards. But Sister Fragrant Garland lived as simply as the poor villagers. She wore shoes, it was true, but they were rough ones woven from raffia. Her brown flax robe was coarse and faded. It wasn't even as nice as the brown cloth of Dawn's blouse. No, he simply could not accept that the nun was a princess, no matter what the adults said.

Then something happened to change his mind. One day while he and his father were digging carrots in the garden near Mrs. Truc's hut, a party of horsemen stopped at the foot of the mountain. A man in regal garb stepped from a horse-driven carriage. Soldiers of the royal guard formed a line on either side of him. He climbed into a sedan chair which two attendants carried up the mountain path. It was a splendid sight. The sedan and carriage were painted vivid red and gold. Loi and his father dared not approach. After digging two bushels of carrots, they stopped by Mrs. Truc's for a drink of water. Mrs. Truc said she had just finished serving tea to the soldiers and they told her that the man riding in the sedan chair was Prince Hue who had come unannounced to visit his sister, the nun. She explained that Prince Hue and Sister Fragrant Garland were both younger siblings of the King.

*...Loi and Dawn helped the nun carry bamboo
baskets down the mountain...*

Loi began to believe that Sister Fragrant Garland was a princess, after all. He made up his mind to visit the convent the next day. He wanted to take a long look at the nun to see what a princess really looked like. The following afternoon he met her on her way down to tend the convent's gardens. He joined his palms in greeting. He found Sister Fragrant Garland as gentle and unassuming as ever. She certainly showed no evidence of having royal blood. Once again, he began to doubt whether she really was a princess. Maybe she was a princess trapped inside the body of a nun, like the prince in the fairy tale trapped inside the body of a frog. Maybe someday Sister Fragrant Garland would change back into a splendid princess. Then he could gaze on her beauty to his heart's content. But this thought filled him with a sudden dread. If she turned back into a princess, would he dare approach her? Would she still call out his name and pat him on the head the way she now did?

One day as Loi and Dawn helped the nun carry bamboo baskets down the mountain to the gardens, he summoned all his courage and asked the nun if she were a princess. She replied, "No, not any longer. Once I was a princess, but now I am an ordinary person like anyone else in Tiger Mountain village."

Dawn asked, "Why did you stop being a princess and become a nun? Weren't you happier being a princess?"

"Being a princess is not as much fun as you children may think," the nun replied. "I am much happier being a nun than I ever was being a princess. If I were still a princess, I would not be able to walk along this mountain path with you. It takes a lot of hard work to be a princess. Just fixing your hair and getting dressed is a major ordeal!"

As he turned these thoughts over in his mind, Loi thought again about the little fish Dawn released that afternoon. According to the fairy tale, a peasant girl named Tam became a queen thanks to a little fish. Could the same thing happen to Dawn? Loi recalled another version of the tale which Sister Fragrant Garland had told him and the other children. She said it was a true story about a queen named Y Lan. Y Lan was born into a simple peasant family. As a child she gathered mulberry leaves and cared for silkworms near the village of Bac Ninh. Her name was Tam and she was very pretty. (Like Dawn, Loi thought.) Tam had a younger half sister by the same mother, whose name was Cam. Cam caught the fish that Tam had kept in the well as a pet, and she cooked and ate it. She buried the bones, but the Buddha appeared to Tam and told her where to find them. He instructed her to bury the bones beneath her bed and to dig them up after one hundred days. She did and to her surprise, found a beautiful pair of slippers. They were a perfect fit. Because they were a bit damp, she left them in the sun to dry. A crow swooped down and carried one off in his beak and dropped it in the palace of King Ly Thanh Tong.

When the King saw the beautiful slipper, he wanted to find its owner. He ordered every young woman in the land to come and try it on. Tam, busy tending mulberry leaves and silkworms, did not hear the edict. Strangely, the slipper fit no one.

That spring, the King travelled by royal carriage to pay respects to the Buddha at Mulberry Pagoda. Everywhere, crowds of people dressed in their finest jostled for a glimpse of the King. As his carriage passed through the village of Bac Ninh, the King saw a young woman picking mulberry leaves. She alone did not join the crowds. He ordered the carriage to a halt and summoned the young woman to him. He asked her why she did not join the others in welcoming him. The diligent and beautiful Tam answered that because her family was very poor she dared not spare a moment from her labor. The King was deeply moved. He asked her to take leave from her family long enough to come to the capital and try on the mysterious slipper. Shortly thereafter, they were married and the King gave her the name Y Lan. He built her a palace and hired a Buddhist scholar to teach her. Queen Y Lan gave birth to a prince who later became King Ly Nhan Tong.

Even though she was a queen, Tam worked as hard as she had in the countryside. She helped her husband rule the country and develop the nation's economy. She arranged affairs at court and oversaw the education of the young. She never distanced herself from the people's hardships. She knew there were thieves in her old village who stole and ate the water buffalo that poor peasants depended on to plow their fields. She asked the King to punish such thieves and to help the peasants by having their debts to wealthy landlords forgiven. In addition, the King ordered that all the children who had been sent to be servants in rich households in order to pay off their parents' debts be allowed to return home. He even helped arrange marriages for some of them.

The people loved their Queen and sang praises of her goodness. They called her the "Daughter of Quan Am, the Bodhisattva of Compassion." Her loving kindness benefited her people. This Tam was not like the Tam in the story Loi's mother told. In Sister Fragrant Garland's story, Tam forgave the sister who ate her pet fish, and she did not hate her mother.

The children loved the nun's story about Tam, and if the nun said it was true, it surely must be. Loi had never known the nun to tell the children anything false. She showed them a book about Queen Y Lan, titled *The History of the Third Queen of the Ly Dynasty*, and told them that in two or three years they would be able to read it on their own. Loi longed for that day. He resolved to study hard. After all, even though Tam had been a very busy queen she still found time to devote to her studies.

Loi understood that it was only thanks to Sister Fragrant Garland that the poorest children in the village were able to go to school. Previously, only children from well-off families had any hope of receiving an education. Wealthy boys looked down on boys like Loi, thinking they had no future. While the rich boys attended school or played, boys like Loi were busy guarding water buffalo, digging potatoes, or catching snails. But now Loi had a chance to study. He had completed the three preliminary reading books in Chinese characters, and started the fourth. Unfortunately, it was becoming harder to find time to study. Since his father's death, Loi was the man of the household and had to assume many more responsibilities. Soon his mother would give birth. Secretly, Loi hoped it would be a little girl as gentle and lovely as Dawn. He would ask his mother to name her Tam and he would catch a fish for her to keep as a pet. Who knows, perhaps one day his own sister might become a princess?

It struck Loi as odd that while Tam changed from a peasant girl into a queen, Sister Fragrant Garland chose to change from a princess into an ordinary person like himself. The thought warmed his heart. His affection for the nun and her protégé, Dawn, refreshed his whole being. In fact, it was thanks to the nun that Loi and Dawn met and became friends. He knew that Dawn scolded him about fishing only because she cared about him. He didn't have many chances to sit and talk with Dawn, but she was never far from his thoughts. She was like a solitary butterfly fluttering over the mustard flowers behind his home. He dared not go too close to the butterfly for fear it would fly away.

Dawn was gentler than he was. She did not catch fish. She killed no living beings, not even snails or insects. Like the nuns, she was a vegetarian. Once Loi found her talking to a rhododendron plant in the convent garden as if it were a small child capable of understanding all her words. First, he thought she was just playing a childish game. But then on another occasion he found Sister Fragrant Garland washing the leaves of a camellia while speaking tenderly to it. He knew the nun wasn't simply playing a childish game, though it struck him as useless. How could plants understand human language? The nun felt his gaze and looked up. She smiled, and answered him as though she could read his thoughts.

"Don't think that plants cannot understand our language or that they do not speak. Plants speak through their leaves and flowers. If we are sensitive enough, we can hear what they are saying. Plants experience sorrow and joy just as we do. See how clever this camellia is to create such perfectly formed flowers! If we love a plant, the plant will love us in return."

Loi loved and respected the nun. He did his best to follow her example. He felt, though, that his bond with the nun was not as close as the bond she shared with Dawn. At times he felt left out. When they sat in the garden together he had the impression that the nun and Dawn dwelled there completely, whereas he was still pulled by the world outside.

With a start, Loi realized that he did not want Dawn to become a princess. If she became a princess, he would never see her. Never again would he carry bamboo baskets down the mountain path with her nor sit by her side in the convent garden. He hoped the little fish rescued by Dawn would not be eaten by anyone. He promised himself that if he ever caught that kind of fish again, he would throw it back into the river. He wanted the nun to remain forever a nun, and Dawn to remain as Dawn. He did not want his baby sister to become a princess either.

Sister Fragrant Garland no longer lived in a splendid palace like Queen Y Lan of long ago, but she was a steady pillar for many people like himself and his mother. Without the nun's intervention, how could his mother have received the medicine she needed? Sister Fragrant Garland's feet must have ached after the many hours of walking to fetch the doctor.

Loi's thoughts were interrupted by a sudden cry followed by Mrs. Tu calling his name. The rice was already cooked, and the pan of water was boiling rapidly. The sky was already light. He hastened to extinguish the fire under the pan and ran into the house. His mother was moaning. Her hands clasped the sides of the bed and her face was beaded in sweat. Mrs. Tu felt her belly, then turned to Loi and said, "Your mother's time has come. Gather some logs and light a fire in the stove. When the smoke is almost gone, bring the charred logs in here. We'll burn the rice husks on the coals to keep your mother warm."

"Is my mother going to be alright?"

"She'll be just fine. Put your mind to rest and get that fire going. A woman's labor is always like this."

Loi gathered some logs and went into the kitchen. He worked quickly. Soon the smoke curled upwards. He heard his mother cry out again. It was a most pitiful cry. Frightened, he ran to her room, but Mrs. Tu chased him out.

"Out in the courtyard with you! Don't come back in until I call you!"

Against his will, Loi returned to the courtyard. His heart felt on fire. He invoked Quan Am's name and prayed that his mother be carried safely through all danger. Fear filled his being. If something happened to his mother, what would he do? He would be completely alone in this world. If only Sister Fragrant Garland was with them, that would calm his fears. Perhaps he should run up to the convent? He hesitated, unsure what to do. No, he must not leave. What if Mrs. Tu needed him to run an urgent errand? It was a long way to the convent. It would be afternoon before he returned. There was no time to summon the nun.

Suddenly Loi heard the convent bell ringing, mingled with the sound of a wooden drum. The celebration for the Buddha's nativity was beginning. Sister Fragrant Garland and the other nuns would be wearing their saffron ceremonial robes. Loi knew a huge congregation was assembled at the convent. Dawn would be there with all the other children to mark the moment the Buddha came into the world. And then, just as suddenly, Loi heard an infant's cry. His mother had given birth! He wanted to rush inside, but he was afraid Mrs. Tu would chase him out again.

He shouted, "Is it alright for me to come in now, Mrs. Tu?"

"Yes, yes, come in!"

Loi dashed inside. His mother looked up at him from her bed and smiled weakly at him. Beside her lay a tiny baby wrapped in an old shirt of his father's. Mrs. Tu was wrapping the afterbirth which she placed in an earthernware pot. She turned to Loi and said, "Your house is very fortunate today. Your mother has just given birth to a fine baby boy. Sit down by your mother while I go out and bury this."

Loi felt his mother's brow and found it cool. He looked lovingly at his little brother. The infant had stopped crying and was already asleep.

"He's really cute, Mother. Do you know what you will name him?"

Loi's mother answered in a thin but happy voice, "Not yet, dear. Mrs. Tu suggested we call him Da, but I was thinking of asking the nun to name him. For now, we will simply call him 'little brother.'"

"You must be very tired and hungry, mother. I'll go down and get you a bowl of hot rice. I'll give you some salted fish with it."

Mrs. Tu walked in at that moment and said, "It will be two or three days before she can eat salted fish. We'll sprinkle some sesame seeds on her rice. Remember, too, that this is the Buddha's nativity, and we should all eat only vegetarian food!"

Loi started down to the kitchen but was stopped by Mrs. Tu. "Don't worry, I can take care of her rice. Why don't you change your clothes and run up to the convent to tell the nun the good news? Go on now, off with you! I can take care of everything here, including building a fire."

Seeing her son hesitate, Loi's mother said, "Do as she says, my child. Go on up to the convent and share our news with the nun. Don't forget to wash your hands and face."

Loi went out behind the kitchen. He undressed and bathed himself by ladling rainwater from a large earthernware vessel. He changed into clean clothes, and took leave of his mother and Mrs. Tu.

As he walked out the gate, he could still hear the slow and distinct cadence of the convent bell. He thought he could hear a faint sound of chanting, but immediately dismissed it as his imagination. Surely it's too far away to hear any chanting, he thought. He wanted to reach the convent quickly, but it was a long climb, and he had time to think about his mother, his new baby brother, and also about Sister Fragrant Garland and Dawn.

Hundreds of birds flew to freedom
accompanied by the people's cheers.

These were the four people he loved most in all the world. He silently prayed to the Bodhisattva of Compassion to keep each of them safe from illness and misfortune.

When Loi arrived at the convent, the recitation of the liturgy was completed and the nuns had returned briefly to their quarters to prepare for the ceremonial bathing of the baby Buddha. The convent was packed. Loi guessed the entire village was there. People were dressed in their best. Loi was the most humbly attired in the crowd. He stood outside the nuns' quarters. They emerged, wearing yellow robes over their usual brown robes. Loi joined his palms and bowed. Sister Fragrant Garland had only to look into his eyes to know that the baby had been born safely.

"Did your mother have a little boy or a little girl?"

"Reverend Sister, my mother has given birth to a boy."

The nun asked Loi to follow her into the formal convent gardens to join the ceremonial bathing of the Buddha. Dawn and the other children were already waiting there, ready to perform the skit they had prepared. All the villagers, children in front and adults in back, surrounded the miniature pond of consecrated water. They moved aside to allow the nuns easy entry. Since Loi was with Sister Fragrant Garland he had no trouble reaching the front.

The people turned towards the statue of the newly born Buddha and joined their palms respectfully. Sister Still Radiance sang the opening verses of the ceremony and then led a recitation of the *Golden Light Sutra*. Though it was a formal ceremony, the atmosphere was more light and cheerful than other days, and everyone chanted with special vigor. After the *Golden Light Sutra*, the nuns recited the Three Refuges and the dedication of merit. At the very moment the dedication was completed, the bird cages were opened and hundreds of birds flew to freedom accompanied by the people's cheers.

"Long live the King, the Supreme Ruler in the land!" exclaimed Sister Still Radiance. With one voice, the congregation responded, "The King!" "Long live the people and land of Dai Viet!" she cried.

Again the people echoed her cry. "Dai Viet!" Their cheers re-sounded up and down the mountain.

Sister Still Radiance continued, "May the people of this land live in peace. May war cease in all four directions. In the realm of living beings, may all wrongdoing cease. May all beings be united on the True Path."

The people exclaimed, "Homage to Shakyamuni Buddha!"

Loi felt an exhilaration he had never felt before. He looked up and saw the released birds flying into the blue sky. Some birds came to rest on overhead branches as though they did not want to leave the ceremony yet. Loi knew that all of these birds had received the Three Refuges that morning. At that moment, Loi's joy was boundless. He wished he, too, could fly with the birds and look down at the happy crowds below.

Sister Fragrant Glory's voice rose above the crowd. "That night Queen Maya had an auspicious dream. She dreamed that a white elephant with six tusks came down from the sky and gently entered her side. When she awoke in the morning, she described the dream to King Suddhodana...."

And so the children's skit began. Draped in a yellow robe, Dawn played the part of Queen Maya. Their friend, Chi, played the part of the King. He invited his soothsayers into the palace, and they predicted the Queen would give birth to a prince who would either become a mighty king or a buddha. The next scene found Queen Maya in the Lumbini grove with two of her atten-dants, played by Thom and Uyen. Dawn grabbed hold of a flow-ering tree branch. Uyen knelt down and lifted the newly-born Buddha, actually a large banana flower wrapped in a piece of yellow silk, from the Queen's side.

The other children sang, "What a joy to be alive on this an-niversary!"

Three small boys playing the part of the Dragon King poured gentle streams of water over the newly-born Buddha. Other chil-dren, representing celestial beings, tossed flowers to celebrate the Prince's birth. Their voices were as bright as sunshine as they sang, "Heavenly music rises, flowers cast from heaven carpet the earth. Greeting the Buddha joyfully, the songs of celestial beings ring out...."

Queen Maya and her attendants returned to the palace.

Behind a large rock, Loi noticed his replacement, Thong, placing a banana-leaf beard over his face to play the part of the old seer Asita. His shoulders were draped in a piece of brown cloth. Loi had a sudden inspiration. He was not too late! He ran behind the rock and when Thong saw him, he understood at once. He removed the beard and cloth and handed them to Loi. He slipped a bamboo staff into Loi's hands. At that moment, a royal guard came on stage to announce that the seer Asita had descended from his hermitage in the Himalayas to seek an audience with the King and to greet the new Prince.

"Summon him in!" Chi commanded in an august voice. Loi stepped out from behind a prop depicting a mountain peak. He leaned on his staff, his back bent with the weight of old age. Slowly he approached the Prince. He gazed on the baby with his bleary eyes. Suddenly his staff trembled and he burst into sobs.

Alarmed, King Suddhodana asked, "Why does Your Reverence weep? Do you see some misfortune that will befall the Prince?"

Loi sobbed a little longer and then raised his head. "Your Majesty, this poor hermit weeps for himself. I am too old and shall not live long enough to see the Prince grow up to become a Buddha. Your Majesty, this infant Prince will one day be a Buddha, a Tathagata...."

Before completing the rest of his speech, Loi stopped to wipe his eyes. As he turned his head, he caught a fleeting glimpse of Sister Fragrant Garland. She was looking straight at him. Clearly, he saw the smile on her lips.

CHAPTER TEN

LIBERATION

Although Young Mountain was a small convent, each nun had distinct duties. As abbess, Sister Still Radiance was responsible for coordinating all convent activities. Sister Peace Blossom was responsible for building maintenance and also served as guest mistress. She supervised all the cleaning, and welcomed all visitors to the convent. When there were more visitors than she could easily handle, Sister Still Radiance and the other nuns lent a hand. Sister Fragrant Glory maintained their library of Buddhist texts, planned their program of studies, and taught the village children. The convent gardens were the responsibility of Sister Fragrant Garland. She tended the flower and vegetable gardens, as well as the convent nursery. The rice field was also her responsibility, but because it was too much work for one person, Sister Still Radiance volunteered to help manage the rice field with help from the Truc family, who lived at the foot of the mountain.

Sister Fragrant Garland planted many syringa shrubs in the convent gardens as well as magnolia, jasmine, rhododendron, and conifers of every sort that flourished on their mountainous terrain. They watered their vegetable garden, located behind their living quarters, with water from a nearby stream. All four nuns assisted in this task. The nursery garden, where Sister Fragrant Garland devoted long hours, was not far from the Trucs' home, and so Mr. Truc frequently assisted her, as did Dawn and Loi. When Sister Fragrant Garland was too occupied with other convent business, Mr. Truc and Dawn carried water for the garden on a carrying pole. Likewise, Mr. Truc and Loi were available to help her carry heavy items.

The summer retreat began on the full moon day of the fourth month and ended on the full moon day of the seventh month. Although the nuns were expected to remain at the convent for the length of the retreat, they were not narrowly restricted. They could go anywhere on the mountain, including down to the convent nursery.

One May morning on their way down the mountain, Sister Fragrant Glory asked Sister Fragrant Garland a question, "I have noticed that the morning office includes the recitation of many *dharani*, or magical formulae. Why is that so, Sister?"

Sister Fragrant Garland had observed the same. Since the day she first heard the novice Dharma Lamp recite the office, she had wondered about the inclusion of such formulae. The office began with the *Surangama Dharani* followed by the *Great Compassion Dharani* and several others. Had the study of meditation in the land of Viet been influenced by the spread of Tibetan Lamaism? After the Mongol invaders made Sung part of their empire, Tibetan Buddhism spread quickly. Although Viet defeated the Mongol army, the influence of their civilization to the north of Viet was still felt. Why didn't the morning office contain more sutras on meditation like the *Lankavatara Sutra* or the *Diamond Sutra*, instead of the dharanis? Sister Fragrant Garland was glad to see that although Sister Fragrant Glory was still young, her insight was sharp. There were few people left, she thought, as astute as this young nun.

Elsewhere in the country, people, without thinking, followed the form of Buddhism practiced across the northern frontier. At large mountain temples, the hierarchy seemed indifferent to this inclusion of lamaistic practices. From her extensive readings, Sister Fragrant Garland knew that Buddhism under the Ly dynasty first prospered, but then declined with the introduction of the "secret teachings" of lamaism. By reading biographies such as *The Life of the Eminent Master Tue Trung,* she learned how Buddhist teachers during the Tran dynasty returned to the original teachings of meditation. To her way of thinking, the study of meditation was being altered by the introduction of lamaism, and she was concerned for the future of Buddhist studies in her homeland. For more than two hundred years, the practice of meditation had been the primary spiritual support for the whole country. Thanks to meditation practice, her homeland had enjoyed peace and had been able to preserve its independence. In recent centuries, the influence of neo-Confucianism, as practiced in the Sung dynasty, had given rise to a schism between Confucianism and Buddhism, not only in the academic world, but in the sphere of politics and at the royal court. Now Buddhism was also being influenced by lamaism. Sister Fragrant Garland wondered whether the Noble Bamboo Forest Teacher had been aware of this development.

Presently, the Bamboo Forest School was producing woodblocks to print a Buddhist canon in Chinese characters. This edition of the canon was being based on an original published under the Mongol dynasty and for that reason contained many sutras referring to lamaistic teachings. As she thought about the printing of this canon, Sister Fragrant Garland's thoughts turned to Bao Sat, the National Teacher. He had been one of the Noble Teacher's foremost disciples. She had been fortunate enough to meet him at Violet Clouds Hermitage on Mount Yen Tu, and again at Self-Blessed Temple in the capital. As National Teacher, he was responsible for printing the Viet canon. Making the woodblocks was a huge undertaking as there were over 6,000 volumes to be printed. The work had begun seventeen years earlier, but had been interrupted when the Noble Teacher died. It was only during the past year that King Anh Tong had issued an imperial decree to resume the work.

The leader of the Bamboo Forest School, Venerable Phap Loa, entrusted this important endeavor to his elder brother in the

Dharma, National Teacher Bao Sat, who was obliged to leave Violet Clouds Hermitage to live at the large Bao An Temple in order to oversee the project.

One hundred artisans worked every day to write and carve the characters on woodblocks. Earlier in the year, Sister Fragrant Garland went to the capital to request that all the Noble Teacher's works be included in this new printing of the canon. She met with Bao Sat who told her that it would be at least another five years before the work was completed. Thus, some works composed by the Viet meditation teachers had been printed and published separately to make them available sooner. These included, among others, *The Life of the Eminent Master Tue Trung*, *Account of the True Essence of the Meditative Mind*, and *Words from the Stone Cave*.

Sister Fragrant Garland understood Bao Sat. She knew he did not desire a life of administrative rank and ritual splendor in the capital. He was the Noble Teacher's best-loved disciple. The only reason the Noble Teacher did not name him the second lineage holder of the Bamboo Forest School was because Bao Sat did not want to shoulder such a responsibility. When Sister Fragrant Garland visited the Noble Teacher on Mount Yen Tu, her father told her to address Bao Sat as an elder brother. Now, despite his high rank, she continued to think of him as a brother.

Sister Fragrant Glory looked at Sister Fragrant Garland, expecting an answer to her question about the dharanis, but she could see that the nun was deep in thought and so she waited patiently for a reply.

Sister Fragrant Garland's thoughts travelled to the time she visited the sacred spots on Mount Yen Tu, in the eighth month of the year 1308. That month, the Noble Teacher sent his students elsewhere and only he and Bao Sat remained on the mountain. Shortly after Sister Fragrant Garland arrived, the Noble Teacher sent Bao Sat on a mission to the capital with a proposal to King Anh Tong that the king prepare to send 300 Champa craftsmen home to Cham as an apology for the abduction of their

Queen Mother. Bao Sat returned within two days, and the three of them set off walking to see the most beautiful sites on the mountain.

Sister Fragrant Garland now understood that her father must have known it would be the last time he would ever make such a walk. He lingered in each place, admiring every tree and touching every slab of stone. They walked for seven days. No site was forgotten. They climbed to the summit and paused at Sleeping Clouds Peak, Violet Clouds Peak, Mortar Hermitage, Medicine Hermitage, Tiger Creek, and other beloved spots. They rested when they were tired and ate a handful of rice when they were hungry. They scooped up cool handfuls of water from the mountain streams to satisfy their thirst. The Princess knew these would always be the most cherished days of her life. They spoke little and demanded nothing of each other, filled as they were with peace, joy, and contentment.

When the Princess took her leave to return to the capital, she had no idea it would be the last time she would ever see her father. She was already making plans to return to the mountain and receive monastic orders from him, after which she hoped to find a beautiful mountain spot with clear water to set up a small convent for practice. The Noble Teacher promised her she could take the bodhisattva vows at the time of her ordination.

How could she have guessed that only two months later, she would receive news of his death? Bao Sat sent messengers to Bao An Temple to announce a period of deep mourning. From the temple, news of the Noble Teacher's death quickly reached the palace. It was an evening early in the eleventh month of 1308. The princess was staying at Self-Blessed Temple with her attendant Pearl. King Anh Tong sent for her and delivered the news that their father had passed away at midnight two days earlier. The Princess returned to her quarters, shut the door, and did not emerge for a day and night. She received no one and refused food and drink. Moreover, she refused to attend her father's funeral rites on Mount Yen Tu with her two brothers, King Anh Tong and

Prince Hue. Three days later, the King returned with Bao Sat to the capital bearing the Noble Teacher's relics. Bao Sat stayed at Self-Blessed Temple for a day and night in order that he might transmit the Noble Teacher's last testament to her. He related to her how the Noble Teacher's final days were spent.

He told her how in the tenth month the Noble Teacher travelled unannounced to the capital to visit privately with his elder sister. He took just one attendant with him, the novice Dharma Lamp. After the meeting with his sister, the Noble Teacher began the return journey with his novice. They stopped to rest one night at Sieu Loai Temple and the next day visited Dharma Clouds Temple. According to Dharma Lamp, the Noble Teacher left a poem inscribed on the temple wall that said,

> *Life's length is one breath,*
> *Moonlight on ocean waves.*
> *Why worry about Mara's realm?*
> *My Buddhaland is the springtime sky.*

The following day they stopped at a nearby convent where the former Queen Mother was living as a nun. She invited him to take the midday meal at the convent. The Noble Teacher accepted the invitation. Smiling, he said, "This may be the last meal I take before *nirvana*." He slept at the convent that night before resuming his journey in the morning. He sent Dharma Lamp ahead and was accompanied by two other novices. When they reached Beautiful Forest Temple on Peace-is-Born Peak, they rested briefly. The Noble Teacher turned to the two novices and said, "I wish to return at once to Sleeping Clouds Hermitage, but there is so little strength left in my legs. How can we manage it?"

"We will carry you, Master," the novices replied, and they carried him up the mountain in a hammock.

When they arrived at Sleeping Clouds Hermitage, the Noble Teacher thanked them and said, "Return down the mountain and apply yourselves diligently to your practice. Don't let birth and death get the better of you!"

Only two attendants were present at Sleeping Clouds, Dharma Lamp and Dharma Emptiness. The Noble Teacher asked Dharma Emptiness to go to Violet Clouds Hermitage and summon Bao Sat.

Bao Sat told Sister Fragrant Garland, "It was nighttime when I received the Noble Teacher's summons, requiring me to wait for daybreak to set off. Then when I was only halfway there, the skies turned dark. Black clouds covered the mountain and torrents of rain poured down. The river rose, making crossing impossible. As night fell, I was forced to take shelter in a mountain hut. My heart felt on fire, and my dreams were filled with strange portents. When I awoke, it had stopped raining and the level of the river had gone down, and I managed to wade across. Thus, I arrived at Sleeping Clouds two days after receiving the Noble Teacher's summons. He said to me, 'I am going away soon. What took you so long to get here? If there is anything in the teachings of Buddhism you have not yet grasped, please ask me now.'

"And so I said, 'In former times when Ma To's attendant saw that the Master was in poor health, he asked him, "How do you feel?" to which the Master replied, "Sun-faced Buddha, moon-faced Buddha." What did the Master mean by that?'

"The Noble Teacher raised his voice in reproach, 'What do you say the five emperors and the three kings were?'

"I responded with another question: 'What is meant by "The flower opens in splendor, displaying colors of great beauty. It is lumber in the North and bamboo in the South?"'

"The Noble Teacher exclaimed, 'Become a blind person!'

"It was then that I knew beyond a doubt how clear he was and how well prepared for his death. This encouraged me greatly. I remained at the hermitage with his two attendants to care for him. We didn't dare venture even a foot from the hermitage. For days it was overcast, and a chilly wind blew. The singing of birds and the calls of owls sounded strangely sad. Then on the new moon night of the eleventh month, the sky cleared and the wind ceased. I went outside and looked up at the sky. There was not a single wisp of cloud, and stars filled the night sky. I went back in and the Noble Teacher asked me the hour.

"'Reverend Sir,' I replied, 'it is midnight.'

"The Noble Teacher raised his hand to push the shutters back. He looked out at the star-filled sky and softly said, 'It is time for me to go.'

"I asked, 'Where does the Noble Teacher need to go at this hour?'

"He recited the gatha,

> *Nothing is ever born,*
> *Nothing is ever destroyed.*
> *If you understand this,*
> *Buddha is before you.*
> *There is no coming or going.*

"I asked, 'What is it like when there is no more birth and death?'

"The Noble Teacher waved his hand and said, 'Speak no more ignorance!'

"Then he sat up in the lion posture and passed from this life. The two novices began to sob. I put my arms around their shoulders and bid them stop. We knelt beside the Noble Teacher's bed and invoked the Buddha's name until daybreak.

"Two days before his death, the Noble Teacher had drawn up a last testament concerning his funeral rites. He did not want a state funeral organized by the royal court. He was a simple monk who practiced on Mount Yen Tu, and he wanted his disciples to perform a simple cremation ceremony. He instructed us to build the funeral pyre right within Sleeping Clouds Hermitage, and to perform the cremation before announcing his death in the capital. To prevent any difficulties or accusations later, he drew up an official will and testament in his own hand, making these requests clear. The novice Dharma Emptiness and I spent the day gathering and chopping fragrant wood for the funeral pyre. That night we placed the Noble Teacher's body on the pyre and lit it. The little hermitage went up in flames. The fragrant perfume of timber floated on the air. We thought we could hear a sound of heavenly music, and we all saw a cloud of five colors drift down and envelop the pyre.

"At daybreak on the following day, I sent Dharma Emptiness to announce the news in the capital. Upon hearing the news, my Dharma brother Phap Loa left immediately for the mountain, as did all the Noble Teacher's students and disciples at Bao An Temple. They arrived the third day after the Noble Teacher's passing. Phap Loa prepared a fragrant infusion to sprinkle over the funeral pyre and performed the ceremony of gathering the sacred relics. The pearl-like stones that had been left in the ashes, 500 in all, filled five containers.

"That evening King Anh Tong, Prince Hue, and all the palace ministers came up the mountain in a solemn procession. They wept and prostrated, until their weeping sound filled the mountain forests. The next morning they descended the mountain. I was obliged to go along in order to give a clear account of all that had happened. We carried the relics of the Noble Teacher to the capital by boat. The ministers did not stop their pitiful weeping. Such a plaintive sound! Some of them expressed displeasure that I had dared perform the cremation ceremony without waiting for authorization from the King. Some even threatened to bring charges against me. I felt no worry. After all, I had merely acted according to the will and testament of the Noble Teacher which I produced for the King to see when we arrived in the capital."

Bao Sat told the Princess that the Noble Teacher had asked him to arrange for her ordination, during which she would be able to take full bodhisattva vows. The Noble Teacher also asked Bao Sat to find a suitable place where she could practice meditation. Bao Sat promised to have his disciple Bao Phac perform the ceremony on Mount Vu Ninh. There the Princess could study with other young students until she had a firm grasp of Buddhist teachings. After that, Bao Phac was to find her an undisturbed place for retreat and practice.

Less than a month later, the Princess took monastic vows on Mount Vu Ninh and began her Buddhist studies with other newly ordained nuns under the direction of Bao Phac. She was given the religious name "Sister Fragrant Garland." Thanks to her intelligent nature, she learned quickly and was much respected by her fellow students. In the tenth month of the following year, she was sent by her meditation teacher to the little convent on Tiger Mountain. She asked to take along her Dharma sister, Sister Fragrant Glory. After three months at Tiger Mountain, they were joined by Sister Still Radiance and Sister Peace Blossom. Because Sister Still Radiance was the eldest and had practiced for more than ten years, Sister Fragrant Garland respectfully invited her to serve as their abbess.

Bao Sat returned to Violet Clouds Hermitage, only to have to leave again to supervise the printing of the canon at Bao An Temple. King Anh Tong conferred the title "National Teacher" on him, as well as on Bao Phac. Sister Fragrant Garland knew that Bao Sat did not care for titles, and the only reason he left Violet Clouds was because no one else could be relied on to publish the canon.

Sister Fragrant Garland knew that Bao Sat's understanding and realization of Buddhist teaching were very deep. She knew he had written the book *Record of the Noble Bamboo Forest Teacher*, even though he had not signed himself as author. The book contained details concerning the Noble Teacher's last days, which Bao Sat had shared personally with the Princess.

As she walked alongside Sister Fragrant Glory, Sister Fragrant Garland appeared deep in thought. She recalled now the conversation between Bao Sat and her father, as he lay on his deathbed. In fact, just the day before, she had been reading that very passage in Bao Sat's book. Reading it, she was struck anew at the deep bond shared by the Noble Teacher and his special disciple.

"When the Meditation Master Ma To was ill, his assistant asked him how he felt, to which he replied, 'Sun-faced Buddha, moon-faced Buddha.'"

Sister Fragrant Garland knew that Bao Sat asked about that exchange, not because he could not penetrate its meaning, but because he wanted to see whether or not the Noble Teacher still dwelled in mindfulness as he prepared to pass from this life. The Noble Teacher, aware of his disciple's intention, answered by scolding him, "What do you think the five emperors and the three kings were?" That was a way of saying that his disciple was underestimating him.

Bao Sat was very content with the Noble Teacher's response, but just to be certain, he asked another question, "...lumber in the North, bamboo in the South...." In telling Bao Sat to become blind, the Noble Teacher was saying that the true essence of things was now as it had always been, arising miraculously and appearing before his eyes. It was another way of saying, "My dear disciple, don't play games with me!"

Sister Fragrant Garland missed her father. She felt especially alone after hearing of the Viet expedition into Champa territory. The foundations of peace and harmony the Noble Teacher had worked so hard to foster and for which the princess had been willing to give her very life, were painfully short-lived. Only three years after the Noble Teacher's death, armed confrontation erupted between the two countries. Three years was just long enough to complete the official period of mourning. Sister Fragrant Garland knew that her two brothers helped lead the war expedition. Did they think of their father as they marched to war? They were his own children, yet rather than fulfilling his hopes, they placed their trust in men who clamored for war. King Anh Tong led a battalion across the plains. Prince Hue led another over the mountains. Naval forces were sent to attack Cham as well.

It was evident that the invasion had been planned well in advance. In fact, promises of support within Cham had been secretly secured from a traitorous Champa commander. In a bid for peace, the young King Harijitputra made the sea voyage from Vijaya to Cau Chiem to perform a ceremony of token submission requested by King Anh Tong. King Harijitputra believed such an act held a true chance for peace and his people's sovereignty. Little did he guess that he would be immediately arrested upon arrival. His younger brother was enthroned by the Viets in a puppet regime. King Harijitputra was escorted under arms to the Viet capital of Thang Long, where he still remained under house arrest at the royal residence of Gia Lam. In an attempt to soften feelings of outrage among the Champa people, King Anh Tong gave the former King the title, "Lord of Loyalty." But of what use are empty titles to deposed kings?

Sister Fragrant Garland knew King Harijitputra well. She understood the young King's kind and honest heart. Perhaps he did not possess the strength and courage of his father, but his loyalty to his people was unquestionable. Although Sister Fragrant Garland knew where King Harijitputra was being held, she resisted a desire to visit him. Questions would surely be raised as to the nature and purpose of such a visit, and, after all, she no longer held any authority. She was far removed from all affairs of the royal court. Furthermore, she feared that such a visit would only add to the bitterness borne by both sides. The peace built by her father now lay in ruins. Champa citizens were taking up arms along the border. What hope remained for peace between their two peoples?

Since his return from the invasion of Cham, Prince Hue no longer came to visit Sister Fragrant Garland on Tiger Mountain. Was he afraid his sister would shame him? No, thought Sister Fragrant Garland, her brother was no more than a puppet himself, too weak to think or act for himself. But what about King Anh Tong? He was not without the intelligence and character to act justly. Sister Fragrant Garland wondered about the influence, wielded over years, of men like Tran Khac Chung, who had led the expedition to kidnap her. She sighed.

But from the depths of her desolation, the nun's spirits suddenly lifted as she thought of people like her Dharma brother Bao Sat. The Noble Teacher had passed from this life, but his work continued. Her heart was warmed by the image of Bao Sat seated at his Violet Clouds Hermitage. And there were still government people who served both in the capital and in the countryside who understood the Way the Noble Teacher tried to show them. Sister Fragrant Garland heard that some ministers at court strongly opposed the invasion of Cham, including the youngest son of the former King Thai Tong. The Noble Teacher's enlightened wisdom and his desire for peace were still present among the people.

Sister Fragrant Garland returned to a deep awareness of her breathing. She felt she breathed for the Noble Teacher as well as for herself. In fact, there was not a moment that she did not breathe the breath of the universally present Noble Teacher. She knew there were many others throughout the country who continued the thread of the Noble Teacher's awakened life. She did not know where the novice Dharma Lamp lived now, but she was sure that wherever he lived, he breathed in unison with the hermit monk who had lived on Mount Yen Tu.

Dharma Lamp would be seventeen or eighteen years old by now, still not old enough to receive full monastic ordination. Yet surely he had progressed far on the path of practice. In her mind's eye she saw the novice dipping his hands in the clear water of the spring. Simultaneously she saw an image of the tiny hands of Loi's newborn brother, whom she had visited two days after his birth. Loi's mother asked her to give the baby a name and she had promised to do so. Loi told her that Mrs. Tu had suggested calling him "Da," but his mother insisted on having the nun name him.

Sister Fragrant Garland thought the name "Da," which meant "Abundance," was a fine name. No doubt, Mrs. Tu held a wish of prosperity and happiness for the baby and his descendants.

The sound "Da" reminded the nun of the name Bud-dha. The baby was born at the very moment the convent bell rang out to hail the Buddha's birth. Another image, as vivid as the mountain river before her and yet as distant as another life, came to her now. It was the image of her own son, Dayada. She did not know where he was now, yet she knew his existence was proof of the bond of friendship, peace, and love once forged. Both these names, Buddha and Dayada, contained the sound Da.

The morning of her visit, Sister Fragrant Garland watched as Loi's mother breastfed her infant son. The image of his tiny hands clutching her breast now became an image for Sister Fragrant Garland of the interdependent nature of all that is. The Lord Buddha, born so long ago in Kapilavastu, was one with the peasant baby pressing his little head against his mother's breast. Dayada's distant image now merged, too, with this village baby. The nun felt that she herself was nursing the baby. She saw that she and Loi's mother were one. She felt as though the milk flowed from her own breast. All false discriminations between noble and humble, past and present, north and south, evaporated like early morning dew in the warmth of the morning sun. The image of the nursing mother enabled the nun to transcend the gulf between birth and death. Sister Fragrant Garland felt like a bird liberated from the net of time, free to fly in the endless freedom of empty space.

Sister Fragrant Garland continued her leisurely pace alongside Sister Fragrant Glory. She understood that Sister Fragrant Glory could not see the illumination awakening in her heart in that very moment. Sister Fragrant Glory had asked her a question about the liturgy and waited for an answer. Sister Fragrant Garland still did not speak. Time disappeared for her. She wanted to find a way to share her sudden bliss and insight with the younger nun but realized that the seeds of wisdom within Sister Fragrant Glory needed more time to mature. For two years now, Sister Fragrant Glory had harbored a desire to visit Mount Yen Tu with Sister

Fragrant Garland. She cherished all the stories Sister Fragrant Garland told her about her time spent with the Noble Teacher and Master Bao Sat on the famous peaks of that mountain. She wanted to taste that same atmosphere, visit every thatched hermitage, every river, stream, and rock. Although other opportunities to make a pilgrimage to the mountain had been offered her, she only wanted to go if Sister Fragrant Garland accompanied her. She believed Sister Fragrant Garland would evoke the atmosphere of days gone by. These were the conditions her heart demanded.

Sister Fragrant Garland, on the other hand, had no desire to return to Mount Yen Tu. She felt it could never be the same without her father's presence. She did not care to see the stupas decorated with gold leaf and precious stones erected in her father's memory. She knew Sleeping Clouds Hermitage no longer existed, though a stupa had been erected on its foundations to house the Noble Teacher's relics. Alongside the stupa, they constructed a new temple. Little Dragon Hermitage had been converted into a pagoda. Many other temples and quarters were built to house the thousands of monks who returned to the mountain for the rainy season retreat each year. Sister Fragrant Garland did not want to lose the feeling of almost supernatural power that the mountain held for her, and so she delayed responding to her sister's request. The only reason she hadn't given an immediate refusal was because she didn't like to disappoint her younger Dharma sister.

The sudden new insights that now flooded her heart caused her understanding to expand. She now saw every tree and every pebble on Tiger Mountain as miraculous and sacred as the trees and pebbles on Mount Yen Tu. The Noble Teacher was present here and now on Tiger Mountain. Dayada was here because the baby Da was here. Buddha was here also. As the Buddha taught, "This is, because that is. This is born, because that is born." Taking care of little Da, she was taking care of Dayada and the newly born Buddha. Da's breathing was the same as the Noble Teacher's breathing, as was the breathing of her younger Dharma sister walking beside her.

Sister Fragrant Garland no longer wanted to refuse her sister's request to visit Mount Yen Tu together. Her attitude had been so narrow in the past! No matter if towers jutted out everywhere along the mountain and visitors crowded every path. The sacred image she held of Mount Yen Tu in her heart could never be spoiled. She would still be able to rediscover the Mount Yen Tu of former days. Yes, she would take Sister Fragrant Glory directly into the Noble Teacher's world, back to Sleeping Clouds Hermitage as it had been. The image she held in her heart was as indestructible as the universal presence of the Noble Teacher.

Sister Fragrant Garland at last broke the silence. "In the eighth month, when the retreat season has ended and there are less people on Mount Yen Tu, I shall take you there."

Sister Fragrant Glory was startled. She had only asked a question about the evening office, yet somehow received the answer to her dreams. She didn't try to figure it out. Her heart swelled with joy. The fact that Sister Fragrant Garland was willing to fulfill her special wish was enough.

And now Sister Fragrant Garland thought about the clouds that gathered above Sleeping Clouds like a halo late every afternoon, as though they were returning to the mountain to sleep....

The monk within the hut does not sleep. He sits in deepest meditation. Earth, rivers, sky, and mountains may be cloaked in the darkness of night, but he sees everything taking place in the capital and along the country's frontiers. With his meditative concentration, he sheds light on all that is happening within and without. The clouds may sleep, but the monk maintains his vigil....

Sister Fragrant Garland felt her whole being tremble. She knew now what name she would give to Loi's newborn baby brother—"Awake."

The clouds may sleep,
but the monk maintains his vigil....

AFTERWORD

Thich Nhat Hanh

Although *Hermitage Among the Clouds* is a fictionalized account, it has the nature of truth and, in many respects, remains very close to historical fact. The dates given for major events all accord with historical fact. I used the book *Tam To Thuc Luc* to supplement much of the information given by other sources, and in some cases used it to correct contradictory information given in other works.

The book *Dai Viet Su Ky Toan Thu*, for instance, states that King Harijit died in the fifth month of the year 1307, but that it wasn't until the tenth month of that year that the Ministers Tran Khac Chung and Dang Van departed for Cham in order "to bring the Princess and Prince Dayada home, because, according to Cham custom, when a king dies, his queen was obliged to be cremated along with him." According to Cham custom, a king's cremation was organized seven days after his death. The delegation leaving from the Viet capital of Thang Long would have arrived six months after King Harijit's body was cremated. Because the Champa feared Viet, it stands to reason that Amazing Jewel was allowed to live until the Viet delegation arrived in order to avoid angering the Viet king. The Champa would certainly have been able to recapture Amazing Jewel after her abduction, for they were exceedingly fine seamen. The above facts suggest to me that they, in fact, allowed her to escape.

It is equally clear that Prince Dayada must have been the son of Amazing Jewel, otherwise why would the King of Viet have ordered Tran Khac Chung and Dang Van to return with the Prince as well as with the Princess? The Champa would have tried to prevent the Prince's abduction because he carried the bloodline of their King, which explains the failure of the ministers to bring him out of Cham.

The book *Dai Viet Su Ky Toan Thu* says of Tran Khac Chung that he "met privately with the Princess and then in haste escaped with her to sea where they spent long days together before reaching the capital." This information is likely the result of gossiping tongues embroidering on the facts. Tran Khac Chung did not travel to Cham alone. He was accompanied by Dang Van, another high official of the Court, and a group of sailors that would have been fairly numerous.

Dai Viet Su Ky also states that after the Noble Bamboo Forest Teacher's death, officials at court demanded the King punish the Buddhist Master Phap Loa for carrying out the cremation ceremony before notifying the King. In fact, the person responsible for the cremation was Buddhist Master Bao Sat. The cremation took place on the second day of the eleventh month, and Phap Loa did not arrive at Mount Yen Tu until the fourth. *Tam To Thuc Luc* makes it clear that the Noble Teacher asked Bao Sat to perform the cremation at Sleeping Clouds Hermitage before announcing his death to the King.

Tam To Thuc Luc says that when Nhan Tong (the Noble Teacher) was born, his eyes were as bright as gold, and he was nicknamed "Golden Buddha" by King Thanh Tong. The author of *Dai Viet Su Ky*, a Chinese-educated scholar who did not care for Buddhism, wrote, "In the palace, everyone called the Prince 'gold of the people.'" It is details like this, though seemingly small, that question the accuracy of the author's account given in *Dai Viet Su Ky*.

I have never visited Tiger Mountain, but thanks to reading the book *Dai Nam Nhat Thong Chi*, I learned that Princess Amazing Jewel practiced as a nun there upon her return from Cham. And thanks to the article *"L'Inscription Chame de Po Sah"* by E.

Aymonier,[*] I learned that the Princess was given the name Paramesvari by King Harijit when she arrived in Cham, and that this was engraved on the Po Sah Stele.

I wrote *Hermitage Among the Clouds* during the time 200,000 Vietnamese soldiers were occupying Cambodia, a situation I found suffocating. One cannot condemn the expansionist acts of others while engaging in expansionist acts. We have no right to condemn imperialist invasion when we ourselves are involved in imperialist invasion. We may wish to condemn others for playing the role of international police, but we should not send hundreds of thousands of our sons and brothers to kill and be killed in another country under the guise of "the national interest." When one knows what suffering is, one should not inflict it on others. Let us be aware of the imperialist blood that runs in our own veins.

The Noble Bamboo Forest Teacher and Princess Amazing Jewel opened their hearts to the Champa people and therefore wished to live in peace with them. Their hearts were able to embrace another people as their own, exchanging a partial love for a greater love. Who does not wish for brotherhood among all the countries of Southeast Asia? But military force will not bring about brotherhood. Only a heart of love can do that.

Many friends and students of mine from overseas have had the chance to visit Vietnam and climb Yen Tu Mountain, the headquarters of the old Bamboo Forest School of Meditation. It would be wonderful if future visitors would read *Hermitage Among the Clouds* before they go. This will serve as a gate for them to enter the sacred mountain where the Noble Teacher practiced.

[*] *Bull. Comm. Archeol. Indochine*, 1911.

CHRONOLOGY

**1225
-1400**   Tran Dynasty.

**1257,
1285,
1287**   Kublai Khan's Mongol forces invaded Viet and were repelled.

1282   Codification of a national written language in which vernacular Vietnamese was represented by a demotic character script called chu nom ("southern writing").

1291   Death of the Eminent Master Tue Trung.

1292   Prince Thuyen (later King Anh Tong) appointed Crown Prince.

1293   Prince Thuyen ascends the throne with the title Anh Tong at the age of eighteen. King Nhan Tong becomes Thai Thuong Hoang, "King Father," or former king. The younger brother of King Anh Tong is given the title Hue Vo Vuong at the age of thirteen years.

Death of Queen Khan Tu.

1295   King Nhan Tong prepares to take monastic orders in the royal country seat Vu Lam.

1299   King Nhan Tong takes monastic orders on Mount Yen Tu, his religious title being Lieu Quan, "Ascetic of Bamboo Forest."

1300   Birth of Prince Manh (son of King Anh Tong).

1301   The Noble Bamboo Forest Teacher goes on a pilgrimage to Cham. He promises his daughter, Princess Amazing Jewel, in marriage to King Harijit.

The festival known as "Boundless Offering" is organized at the Pho Min Temple, a festival for giving religious teachings as well as for the distribution of food, money, and clothes to the poor.

1304   The Noble Teacher goes out among the people, teaching Buddhism and counseling the practice of the Ten Precepts.

        The Noble Teacher ordains Phap Loa (the second lineage holder of the Bamboo Forest School).

        King Anh Tong receives the Five Precepts.

1305   Phap Loa receives full monastic orders at Ky Lan Monastery.

        Huyen Quang (third lineage holder of the Bamboo Forest School) is ordained by Bao Phac.

        The Champa ambassador comes to Viet to perform a marriage proposal ceremony for Princess Amazing Jewel.

1306   Phap Loa is appointed Master of Studies at Sieu Loai Temple.

        Bao Phac brings Huyen Quang to the Noble Teacher to act as his attendant.

        Princess Amazing Jewel goes to Cham.

1307   The Noble Teacher spends the rainy-season retreat at Sleeping Clouds Hermitage and teaches *The Record of Great Wisdom* to Phap Loa and other disciples.

        The two lands of O and Ri are annexed to Viet.

        Death of King Harijit.

        Two ministers, Tran Khac Chung and Dang Van, go to Cham to rescue the Princess, fearing she will be burned on the funeral pyre.

1308   The Noble Teacher performs the Ceremony of Transmission to Phap Loa and appoints him incumbent abbot of Bao An Temple, in the presence of King Anh Tong and the court.

        The Queen Mother, Tuyen Tu, takes monastic orders and receives the bodhisattva vows from Phap Loa.

        Princess Amazing Jewel returns home.

        Death of the Noble Teacher. Bao Sat performs the cremation ceremony at Sleeping Clouds Hermitage.

        Phap Loa writes the foreword to the book *Words from the Stone Cave*, by the Noble Teacher.

1309   Conveyance of the relics of the Noble Teacher from Self-Blessed Temple in the capital to the stupa on Mount Yen Tu. A large offering ceremony is organized in the name of the Noble Teacher.

1311   King Anh Tong invites Phap Loa to Self-Blessed Temple in the capital to teach *The Record of Great Wisdom*. The King delegates Phap Loa to distribute money and silk to the poor.

1313   Death of King Harijitputra in the Gia Lam country palace.

King Anh Tong designates Bao An Temple as the headquarters of Buddhist practice in the country. He orders the setting up of a registry of all monks and nuns in the country and stipulates the duties of the ordained throughout the land.

Queen Bao Tu gives 300 acres of rice fields to Bao An Temple.

1314   The Buddhist Canon is finally completed. The printing blocks are stored in Bao An Temple, a complex of seventy buildings, including a Buddha Hall, sutra library, and residences for the ordained.

Prince Manh ascends the throne with the name King Minh Tong, at the age of fifteen.

1316   King Anh Tong receives the lay bodhisattva precepts.

1317   Prince Hue is sent to Cham to make war.

The younger brother of King Harijitputra flees to Java, his mother's homeland.

1318   Former King Anh Tong invites Phap Loa to the shrine in Thien Truong Palace to give commentaries on Buddhist teachings. King Anh Tong gives Phap Loa the title "Universal Wisdom."

King Minh Tong summons an Indian monk to translate the Bach Tan Cai Dharani Sutra.

Death of the Queen Mother Tuyen Tu.

1319   Famine. King Minh Tong requests Phap Loa to organize a relief operation.

Prince Hue invites Phap Loa to An Hoa Palace to teach *The Record of Great Wisdom*.

1320   Death of former King Anh Tong.

1321   Hoai Ninh casts a statue of Quan Am Bodhisattva with 1,000 arms and eyes, and writes the dedication for the Viet canon.

Prince Hue takes the lay bodhisattva precepts at Sung Nghiem Pagoda.

1322   Phap Loa writes the book *Guide to Meditation Practice*, published under the pen name Minh Giac.

The Bamboo Forest School casts 1,000 Buddha statues.

Lord Van Hue Vuong is ordained a monk by Phap Loa.

1324   Quynh Lam Temple has more than 1,000 acres of rice fields and 1,000
       laborers to work the land.

       Lord Hue Tuc Vuong leads an invasion of Cham and is defeated. He
       is forced to withdraw his army and Cham's independence is restored.

1330   Death of Phap Loa.

1377   King Due Tong invades Cham. He is ambushed and dies in the town
       of Tra Ban. The Viet army is heavily defeated. At the end of the year,
       the warship Che Bong Nga reaches Thang Long, the Viet capital.

Parallax Press publishes books and tapes on mindful awareness and social responsibility. We have published several books on Vietnamese culture and history, including *The Moon Bamboo* and *A Taste of Earth and Other Legends of Vietnam*. For a copy of our complete catalog, please write to:

Parallax Press
P.O. Box 7355
Berkeley, CA 94707

La Boi Press has available all of Thich Nhat Hanh's books in Vietnamese. For a copy of their complete list of titles, please write to:

La Boi Press
P.O. Box 781
San Jose, CA 95106